Before Now

A NOVEL BY

NORAH OLSON

KT KATHERINE TEGEN BOOKS
An Imprint of HarperCollinsPublishers

Katherine Tegen Books is an imprint of HarperCollins Publishers.

ISBN 978-0-06-234707-7

Typography by David Curtis
17 18 19 20 21 PC/LSCH 10 9 8 7 6 5 4 3 2 1
❖
First Edition

For Birdie

Cut him out in little stars,

And he will make the face of heaven so fine

That all the world will be in love with night

And pay no worship to the garish sun.

—William Shakespeare

9/3, NIGHT

The air smells different today. Clean. Sharp. Light. The stale, humid weight of the Midwestern summer is past, and I'm sitting on the roof again, back home under a fragile pale-blue sky. Writing for the first time since I saw the ocean. When the wind blows, I can taste the first day of autumn drifting in off the lakes.

Before all this, I dreamed of disappearing. I dreamed of other worlds. I dreamed of the comfort of astronomical distances, exactness, blackness. The relentless life of light.

Now, there are no more dreams.

Months have passed, but I can still hear the waves breaking, the hush of the ocean rushing onto the beach. I can smell the rotting seaweed and feel the bite of sand fleas, my shirt wet, cold, and stuck fast to my skin. A bitter taste of salt water on my tongue, sand in my mouth, grinding between my teeth.

I remember lying in a room afterward with my eyes closed, knowing that I wasn't dead. Hoping I would see Cole's eyes looking back at me, knowing that I wouldn't. A faint, steady beep marked each beat of my heart, and I felt the tangle of wire across my chest, the dull ache of the IV needle in my vein. I reached up and held the tiny golden sun that rested on a thin chain around my neck.

When I opened my eyes my father was there, and he spoke to me.

"Atty."

His voice was soft and full. Salt water streamed from his round dark eyes as he said my name through a pained smile.

"I am so sorry," he said.

I looked up from the cold hospital bed at Papa, smiling weakly through the tears. He squeezed my hand.

"We'll go back," I said, "and start again."

I didn't know how long it had been since they'd found me on the beach. But even through the thick haze inside my head, I did remember how it felt.

The tide had gone out, and it was either early morning or dusk. I had no idea. My mouth was dry, my skin sunburned. The sand felt like fire. Above me in the half-light, a man whose face was hidden by shadows was saying something I couldn't understand. His hand pressed firmly under my jaw. He looked at his watch as orange and red lights flashed around me, illuminating the air in short, sharp bursts.

I rolled my head to the side and saw Cole lying still,

next to me on the beach. His face was swollen, his body cold and hard like something locked. A box snapped shut. I wanted to press my cheek against his. Feel his skin touch mine. His once-beautiful lips were crusted with sand, an eye half open, swollen, unseeing, sun-scorched. *I will correct this mistake* was all I could think; something frantic in my head like a rat running on a wheel, trying to keep ahead of the terror.

And then I felt it, the slow and terrible wail that'd been building in my belly for years, maybe my whole life. But no noise passed through my chapped and bleeding lips. My scalp was gritty, and sand was caked to my face. I opened my mouth to scream or beg whatever forces in the universe had separated us, but it was as if all the air in the world had been sucked away, all noise extinguished. And all I could do was lie there and gasp. I knew the drugs were still working because I couldn't stand or kneel or even lift my hand. A crushing, hollow pain came out of nowhere. The ocean roared and broke beyond the cliffs. But I was as silent as the boy in the sand. As silent as death.

Two more medics dressed in blue shorts and white shirts slid Cole's body onto a stretcher, and he was gone. From somewhere behind the fog in my head a horrifying thought was forming, rolling in to engulf me. The panic of the amnesiac, of the coconspirator, of the failure. We did not make it to Mexico. We did not leave this Earth together.

I was nowhere, but alive and alone.

6/8, NIGHT

Sitting on a piece of driftwood, looking out at the water. The sea glitters with the reflection of a thousand stars. I am calm as I write these words in the moonlight. My last words. Our last words.

We took all the pills. One or two at a time so we wouldn't throw them up, until we finished the last of forty; sitting, looking out at the reflection of the stars in the black Pacific Ocean, watching the white-tipped waves gently kiss the land. I gave Cole six extra of mine; he asked for them because he's bigger and weighs more. We'll never see Mexico, but we'll be together. Always.

I can't feel any of it yet, but soon it will be all I can feel.

I want you, whoever finds this journal, to know we were happy. We are happy. We've made our decision—the only choice we really had. People think suicide is for people who hate themselves.

But they don't understand.

This was not an act of annihilation.

This was an act of self-love, of protection.

We would rather die than pay for other people's crimes.

My father would never understand this. The way he insists he's seen everything just because he's a cop, but he couldn't even see what was going on right in front of his own eyes. He thinks he's the one who experienced all the adversity because he's an immigrant, came up from nothing, that he can sit and tell everyone what to do. Not just me and Cole, but *everyone* has to follow his rules. And I'm supposed to achieve all the things he couldn't. I'm supposed to be in all the honors classes, not because I like it or I want to learn, but because it'll show everyone who our family really is.

He cares so much about how people see us. He pretends he's got working-class pride, but he has working-class shame. "*They* see us as trash," or "*they* discriminated against us." But then he discriminates against Cole! Hates Cole. My mother wanted me to be with some good Christian boy whose parents are doctors or lawyers and who live up in Edina in some fancy house, like if I did that I would be winning something for them. Ridiculous! Like any of those country club boys in the Minneapolis suburbs would date a brown girl named Atabei Taton. If they'd really wanted even a chance for it to be different they would have named me Abby or Emily or Hannah.

Cole and I were their worst nightmare. I found a boy

from the building. A white boy whose family is always in trouble with the law. And my father, dutifully sworn to "protect and serve," couldn't stand the idea that I would spend even a moment in their apartment. He would come back after patrolling in Hawthorne or Longfellow saying things like "I saw the mother of that boy wandering down Pacific Street today—you know it will come to no good."

As if that had anything to do with Cole.

Cole tried to comfort me, but it didn't work. I'm too angry. Too scared that at any moment the police will come find us and take us back, that some do-gooder will walk down the beach with her golden retriever, recognize us from a "missing" poster at the supermarket, and turn us in.

Cole talked about his mother, and it made me feel selfish. I shut up because I know I'm lucky compared to him. His mom, Jennifer—he never called her Mom—nodding out on the couch or rifling through kitchen drawers looking for a few hidden dollars to pay for dope.

He is the only person I have ever met who gets it about freedom. Because if there's anyone who has experienced adversity, it's Cole. But they will hunt us down and take him away for something he did for me, things he did for his mother. Assault and battery. Selling drugs. Missed court dates and broken probation. Accused of kidnapping! Half of it isn't true. None of it's his fault. And the people who really deserve to be locked away are walking around free. Are seen as respectable.

Here, on our hidden beach, our last chance to be ourselves.

Before we took the pills, I stood knee-deep in the water, my back to Japan and the expanse of ocean in between, watching Cole twist something in his fingers by the shore.

"Atty, look out!" he called.

For a second I thought that we had been caught! But then I was knocked forward by a six-foot wave that sent me sprawling to his feet, spun head over heels like clothes in a washing machine. Cole's head lifted up, and he laughed so loud that I panicked and thought for sure someone would find us. But the thought passed, and I stood, covered in seaweed like an old movie monster. I rushed at Cole and knocked him down, grabbing him around his chest. He rolled me around the sand, his arms gentle and strong. We laughed, gulping down air and pressing against each other until we landed intertwined along the water's edge.

"Look," he said suddenly. "I made this for you."

Cupped in the palm of his hand was a tiny braided ring made of rope strands that had washed up on shore. Round and delicate and perfect. I slid it onto my left index finger and kissed him, tasting the sweetness of his breath.

6/8, EVENING

'm on the sand, tucked under Cole's arm. Finally still after all the running. It's dark and I can hardly see the page, but I'm writing anyway. Thinking about the lifetime that we've lived in one day, from the top of the Ferris wheel at the Las Vegas Speedway to the end of our world on the beach of the Pacific.

It was just minutes ago, but now that the decision is made, it seems like we were different people before. We were sitting on a wide, flat rock at the very edge of the cliff. The car was next to us, doors open, radio on. The breeze blew gently and ruffled our thoughts as we looked at the endless expanse of water.

"I think I can see Japan," Cole joked.

I smiled and thought about all the space between here and there. The time it takes to travel distances. It had been days since I'd had any real sleep, and my body was humming from exhaustion, from adrenaline, fear, excitement. How much longer were we going to have to hide? How long would it take to get to Mexico? And when we get there, how will we ever get across the border?

Below us the Pacific smashed itself against the packed earth of the sheer cliff, white foam sprayed up the side, and the undertow made a hideous sucking sound as the water pulled back over sharp black boulders. Four gray pelicans flew low over the waves.

Strange Mexican accordion ballads wafted toward us from the car, then the local news; a new eco container unveiled at the San Diego County Fair, three San Dieguito youth softball all-star teams reach the state finals, Fairy Festival starts July 6. We giggled as the announcer paused but caught our breath when he said: "In breaking news: the California Highway Patrol reports that a missing Minnesota girl and her abductor were spotted traveling south on Interstate Fifteen near the town of Barstow earlier today in a white 1997 Volkswagen Jetta, California license plate number 6DZG263. If sighted, call nine-one-one immediately, as the suspect is considered dangerous."

I sprang up as if an electric current were running through me, and I suddenly saw the world through the wrong end of a telescope. I turned off the radio and looked at Cole, still standing by the boulder at the edge of the cliff. He seemed a million miles away.

The only sound was the white noise of the surf advancing

and retreating below us. "That tollbooth operator. She called it in!"

"We can't let them catch us," he said, his voice rising.

"There's no way that I'm going back. Not now! Not ever."

A chill ran up my spine, and before I could hesitate or think I was in motion. I knew what I had to do. I'd hurl myself off the end of the continent—smash my head open into shards of bone and blood and flesh. I belonged to no one, and they would never have me. The whole world went white, and I dug my heels into the ground. Ran toward the setting sun.

I didn't see Cole. But with a jolt I felt his shoulder against my ribs, his arms wrapping around my waist. He knocked me down and landed on top of me. We skidded along the earth, kicking sandy gravel off the cliff's edge. My foot dangled in the air high above the water.

Cole held me tight. I cried.

I felt his breath hot and moist in my ear as he held me under my arms and dragged me from the cliff's edge. I didn't struggle. Though I breathed, my body felt lifeless. I had no more energy. No more fight.

We collapsed on the ground and leaned against the side of the car facing the ocean.

"Not like this," he whispered to me as I cried. "Not like this."

Cole reached across me and pulled the pencil box full of pills from his bag. He pulled out four blister packs, and I understood.

We rolled the stolen car under a low leafy tree, just out of sight, and walked down a set of weather-beaten steps that led to the water. The last bit of sun dipped below the horizon as we stepped into the darkness below. Then the wail of a siren stopped us dead in our tracks. As the sound got closer I squeezed Cole's hand, not daring to breathe. They're still searching—but out here, on foot in the blurry dusk, they won't find us.

On the beach, around a bend in the shore, it was dark and quiet. No houses, no people, no parents, no police. We were alone. Cole put his hand on my cheek, and I felt the universe expanding, slowly, over millennia. I looked him in the eye and kissed him: happy, trembling. The tide was pulling out toward where the sun had disappeared below the far edge of the waves, and in the half-light Cole's arm circled my waist.

"There." I pointed to the darkened sky above us. "Andromeda. Just think, inside that little blur is a whole galaxy."

"Mm-hmm," he hummed. "Whole worlds floating around that dusty cloud, waiting to collide."

I could feel the warmth of his chest against my bare skin. The air still held the heat of the sun as our bodies pressed against each other on the cool, densely packed sand. Cole's skin was smooth beneath my fingers, his body perfect next to mine. I imagined our stars burning brightly until they extinguished themselves, leaving behind a flash of light traveling slowly across the night sky.

And now, nothing has *any* power over us—not the police, not our parents, not even death. We've outrun the first two, embraced the last. Here on the beach, we'll win this race. We'll get away to a place where no one will follow.

Dream:

My father is looking at me, his face wide-open, his expression questioning and thoughtful. My father, his round dark eyes, his high forehead and strong nose. He is calling me *ti chouchou*, as always, in that Creole accent. He still has his uniform on, but he's locked the gun in the safe. "Here, *ti chouchou*, let me see. I won't be mad. We can fix it."

I've broken the telescope. But I can't tell him.

I can see through his shirt, and through his skin. His heart is beating so fast I'm afraid it will burst.

I hand him the scope and when he holds it up to the sky I can see what he sees. There among the farthest stars I am floating. Giving off heat. Absorbing the darkness around me. Emanating light.

Memory:

We were driving along the foothills of a mountain range, Utah, maybe Nevada, and the road had been empty of all signs of life for hours. Cole dozed while I drove. I was wide-awake from fear and an eagerness to get past it all. He was angelic—head tilted back, thin lips slightly parted, all the lines smoothed out of his face as he slept—a perfect being. His dirty-blond hair, cut short just days ago, was matted down against the headrest, and I stole glances at his features—the thick lines of his brow above dark eyelids shielding his light-blue eyes; his long, smooth nose between high cheekbones and square jaw; five days' worth of downy beard on his chin gave way to a neck so smooth I wanted to press my mouth against it.

He awoke woozy and peered out into the lightless landscape as we sped along. He wanted to pull over. Turn off the headlights. See the clear, deep night sky. He was thinking about the telescope sitting in the trunk, but all I could think of was the end of Bonnie and Clyde, ambushed by the Feds from the roadside after running from every kind of law officer. One hundred sixty-seven bullet holes in the car—fifty-three in Bonnie, slumped over in the driver's seat; fifty-one in Clyde, lying motionless in the dirt. I didn't want to stop in the middle of nowhere, our pictures all over TV and Facebook and Twitter. Minors gone missing; Cole wanted for kidnapping, car theft, assault and battery, violating probation. Then I looked out the side window and saw the night. I took in a deep breath. Yes, let's stop. Let's look. It may be our last chance.

Fact:
As an object travels closer to the speed of light, it experiences time at a much slower rate.

6/8, LATE AFTERNOON

The ocean! At last. I'm sitting in the sand, writing, watching Cole chase sandpipers back and forth along the breaking waves. Two thousand miles away from Hennepin Avenue in Minneapolis, and no one behind us. We've outrun them all.

We'd been speeding for days in a blur of asphalt and trees, taking turns sleeping and driving, the mile markers rushing past, Cole's head leaning against the passenger window. I wanted to lick the saliva from the corner of his lips as he slept, but dying in a heap of steel and glass without ever having put my feet in the ocean wasn't what I had in mind.

Around a bend in the road, at the edge of a cliff—more water than I'd ever seen in my sixteen years on Earth.

Impossible in its scale. Endless.

I pulled over and nearly wept from the beauty of it. From the fact that I was finally here.

Then Cole was awake.

"Atty, it's just amazing," he said. "How can it be . . . ?"

"So vast?"

"So dark."

We drove farther, winding our way down the coast, and found a place to park.

"Here."

I carefully slid the Jetta beneath a wide and ancient-looking avocado tree. We were on a leafy street that dead-ended at a stand of eucalyptus trees above the ocean, where orange-and-black butterflies fluttered in the sunlight. The small wooden bungalows that dotted both sides of the road were hidden by tall bushes or exposed by small grassy lawns littered with red wagons and plastic climbing toys.

"Perfect," Cole said. The slightest tremor in his voice.

The little Volkswagen I had hot-wired in Nevada fit right in here among the vintage rebuilt Fords and old Subaru station wagons with surfboards attached to the roofs.

The clap of the car doors closing behind us sounded like gunshots in my ear. Cole flinched. But the street was quiet. We were walking without speaking, holding hands, when I tripped on a lumpy tree root that was pushing up the concrete. Cole grabbed my arm and kept me from falling flat on my face.

"Watch it!" The thin, gravelly voice rang out of the dark and made us jump.

"I keep *telling* the landlord 'someone's gonna kill

themselves on that thing one day,' but he *never* listens!"

We looked in the direction that it came from and saw a small redwood-shingled house with a low shaded porch. In the shadows I could make out the slight figure of a woman with gray hair all tied up in a bun. She sat in a chair. Rocking slowly.

My pulse thundered in my ears and I barely managed a weak "Oh, yeah. I'm okay."

Cole nodded his head and waved in her direction.

We walked to the end of the street and through the trees. After a minute, Cole said, "I hope she doesn't watch TV."

We headed down toward the beach and found a secluded spot to look out at the ocean, to be still and alone. I touched the back of his neck with my fingertip, then put my mouth just below his jawbone. The salt smell of the ocean mixed with the dried sweat on our skin, and I nearly collapsed from the burning sensation inside of me. When I kissed him, I knew that we had made the right decision to run away. The sleepless nights, the narrow escapes—there was no reason to turn back, then or now.

Our bodies pressed together, and my skin was alive. Inside I shook as the forces of this world shot through me. The white noise of the surf filled my ears, and warmth radiated from each cell of my being.

6/8, AFTERNOON

We were somewhere around Barstow at the edge of the desert when reality started to kick in.

California!

Not much farther to Mexico now. We're getting away, like Bonnie and Clyde. The sun was straight up above us, and it must have been a hundred degrees on the ground. Just a few more hours to the coast, and I could hardly sit still! Yes. We can outrun the highway patrol, our parents, and that goddamn Daniel White. Cole was bouncing up and down in the driver's seat to the Astrix remix that was blasting out of the dashboard, and I was trying not to think too much about getting caught. Trying not to think about what they'd do to Cole.

At the tollbooth where the highways merged, we pulled into the cash lane and asked the operator for directions. Told her we're going to the beach! Can't wait to swim in that ocean. Taste the salt in our mouths. Feel the cool, wet sand between our toes.

"Well . . ." She smiled. "Take I-15 down to Corona, then hit 91 West till I-5. Somewhere around the San Juan Capistrano turnoff, you'll be sure to see the water."

She had a look on her face as if she were envious; stuck out here in the middle of nowhere, sitting in a little shack on the highway with nothing but a cash register and a little TV tuned to some old reruns, listening to her favorite songs from her tiny iPod speaker over and over again.

Not for me. Not for us. Cole and I, we're going to see the ocean, turn left toward Mexico, and disappear.

"You kids been driving far?"

Cole hesitated for a second and said, "Las Vegas. But before that, Phoenix. That's where we're from."

"Phoenix, eh? My husband's from there. We go back every so often. His mom's still down there in a little community called Estrella Village. Real pretty. You can see the mountains from her window. You know the place?"

Cole shifted in his seat. "Um, Estrella Village, hmmm . . . oh, sure. By the mountains, yeah. We live downtown, so we don't get out that way much."

"Oh." The tollbooth woman gave us a hard look, then said, "Have fun at the beach. You're heading the right way."

We waved and drove slowly out of the toll plaza without saying a word. To the side was a low, flat concrete building. Two highway patrol cars were parked out front.

"That sucked," Cole said in a low voice. He punched the steering wheel in frustration and accelerated onto the freeway.

We came up quickly to the first exit, and I pointed to the sign. Cole turned us off and drove along the service road and into a dusty two-pump gas station. I filled the car while he went in and returned with an old-school road map of Southern California.

"She'll tell the cops which way we went," he said. "We'd be easy to pick off on the highway. Let's go south and take the county roads."

The cashier was watching us from inside his little bulletproof glass booth.

"I'll drive," I said. I was nervous, thinking about how far we'd come. Feeling trapped and watched by everyone.

On the overpass across the highway I wondered if we'd really make it. But we had to. We'd gone so far beyond the point of turning back.

Dream:

I float. The deep darkness of space is all around me, but at the edge of my vision a million fiery suns burn brightly. There is no sound. A quiet like none I've experienced before. My nose tingles, and I can smell the earthy scent of Cole's body, but I am alone. My body is warm, and I am breathing freely, though I can feel the vacuum of space all around me, fantastically cold. I begin to tumble in the weightlessness.

What starts as a slow, high, arcing somersault—the universe turning head over heels—becomes faster and tighter, until a few minutes later I am being washed through space at a dizzying speed. The stars are lights spinning like the small bulbs on the roof of a carousel gone out of control. The starlights blur together, giving off a white glow that grows until it covers everything, until it blinds me.

Memory:
Thinking of that day at Cole's house, back home, before we left.

Jennifer came to the door wearing light-blue jeans torn at both knees and a purple V-neck T-shirt that looked about three sizes too big. Her skin had a sickly greenish tint to it, and her eyes had very fine lines around them in all directions, with dark, purplish semicircles beneath. She smiled at me and gave me the once-over, pausing at my hair and my bracelets. "Come on in, sweetheart," she said. "Cole's in the kitchen."

It was the first time that I had been in their kitchen, and I was surprised at how empty it was. Fridge, counter, sink, cabinets, and stove, of course, but that was it. No table, no clock, no pictures on the wall or plants in the window. A round fluorescent bulb cast a bluish light over the room. Definitely depressing. Upstairs in our apartment, the kitchen is my favorite room in the house; always warm and bright, with leftover smells of fry bread or slow-cooked stew and a sturdy wooden table that Papa had gotten at yard sale in St. Paul.

My face must have shown my thoughts, because the first thing Cole said was "Yeah, it's not much to look at in here, huh?" It was true, but it had been such a great day and I was so happy to be there with him that it didn't matter. I kissed him, and his face relaxed. I found a pot in a cabinet and put some water on to boil. Jennifer leaned in the doorway and talked, told us about dinners her mother made.

We ate in the living room. Cole and I sat on the floor with plates on our laps, Jennifer sat on the couch. I guessed something happened to the coffee table since I was there last time—there was no other furniture in the room.

I talked about the trip to the observatory when she asked about school, and told her about EDM when she asked about my bracelets. Jennifer talked about rock music from the '90s, a bunch of bands that I had never heard of, going to see the punk shows at 7th Street Entry. She asked me about my name, saying, "Atty. It's so pretty, where's it from?"

And that's where it all went wrong.

As I was talking about Haiti and Red Lake Nation I could see her face growing darker, closing in on itself. God, I thought, and braced myself for some backhanded racist bullshit. As soon as I told her my last name was Taton she had a total freakout—her plate hit the floor and broke into three large chunks; she stood up, red-faced, and for a minute I was actually afraid she'd hit me.

"You're the daughter of that son of a bitch pig that lives upstairs! Cole, you just thought you'd leave that part out? You thought you'd leave out the part about her father harassing me, trying to call child welfare on me? What are you doing with this girl?" She turned to me and growled. "What are you, a little spy?"

Cole looked as shocked as I felt.

"Mom, stop it. Officer Taton has given us a lot of breaks." He tried to stand in between us.

"GET OUT!" she screamed at me. "GET OUT OF MY HOUSE!" She was standing on the couch, pointing at the door. "Don't you ever come back here! Don't you *ever* talk to my son again! You are a *spy*, aren't you? Trying to seduce my son so you can find out if I'm clean or not. He sent you here to spy on me! Goddamn all of you straight to hell!"

It looked like she was about to pounce on me. Cole jumped up and held her around the waist shouting, "Mom! Mom!"

I didn't wait around to find out what might happen next.

Fact:
A day on Mercury is fifty-nine times longer than a day on Earth.

6/8, MORNING

It was still dark when we drove through downtown Las Vegas, oblivious to the gamblers and tourists who wandered the streets. A sign read: Welcome to Paradise. Down a short stretch of dusty road, and we had crossed over into California.

Minnesota had seemed like a wasteland, but this place was truly desolate. Desert. Real desert. Sand and cactus and little rats scurrying across the bubbling hot blacktop. By the afternoon we'll be looking at white waves crashing on the beach. The shitty cornfields and cookie-cutter sprawl of the plains couldn't be farther away.

And the sky. The night stars hang so low out here, I could touch them if only my arms could reach.

I sat on the ground, leaning against the side of the car, writing about how we stole the Jetta. An old noisy truck lumbered past us, and it seemed to take forever to go by. In our stupor, we were terrified that the driver would recognize us, call the police. The headlights left a pattern of light behind my eyelids when I closed them, and I couldn't tell if I'd been sitting there for five minutes or five hours. It was hard to know because we don't have a watch or a cell phone. And I am part delirious from the trip, part intoxicated from finally being all alone with Cole.

He hummed softly to himself as he brought out his old pencil box, covered with stickers that read stuff like *Good job!* and *Wow!* and *Looking up!* Cole smiled darkly at me, and we laughed unsnapping it. He opened it and spilled the contents out onto his lap. In the light of the open door, he read each stamped package intently: donepezil, galantamine, propanolol, sertraline. A whole pharmacopeia instead of school supplies.

The smile faded from Cole's face as he handled the pills.

"Jennifer's," he said.

I must have had a puzzled look on my face, because then he explained. "Some are harmless, but others . . . I thought that if she took some of these on top of the heroin, she'd get sick." His features smoothed out, and his eyes unfocused. "Maybe kill herself by accident."

With a tiny jerk of his head he blinked and went back to looking through the box.

"Here it is."

He held up a blister sheet of little white pills. There were at least three more sheets in the box. Tramadol. I read the label: *one hundred milligram tablets.*

"We have to keep moving until they stop looking," he said. "If we need some money along the way, we can definitely sell these."

Cole rolled the package between his fingers. "It's a pain-killer, makes the world disappear. But if you take too many, you go to sleep." He looked out at the road. "And you don't wake up."

6/8, SUNRISE

ole grabbed the few things we had left in the Prius, and we made our way through the dark fringes of the parking area, checking doors on older-model cars to see if any were open. It only took half an hour and bingo! An ancient Volkswagen Jetta with a sunroof and California plates.

"You want to give it a shot this time?" Cole asked.

I did. I wanted something technical to focus on to calm me. He knew me too well. Cole explained how he'd hot-wired Rita's car when we stole it back home, and I got to work while he sat on the passenger side, grinning as if we had all the time in the world.

It took me three tries, but when the car started, it was thrilling! I gave a little shriek of excitement.

"Atty Taton, you are the smartest, coolest, toughest person I've ever known," he said. "I want to scream your name to the stars."

"Do it," I said.

"Atty Taton!" he screamed, his head out the window as I drove fast along the outside of the speedway. The gray light of dawn was creeping over the sky. "Atabei Taton, I love you! I love you! I love you!"

6/8, BEFORE DAWN

Sitting on the concrete outside the Las Vegas Speed-way, catching our breath. It must be almost morning. Drenched in sweat, heart pounding, head soaring. The first time that I've sat down in almost five hours. The deep desert sky is flashing violet, magenta, lime, cobalt. There isn't a star to be seen, and when I look up the whole ground goes sideways like I'm back on the Tilt-A-Whirl. The earth hums, and my stomach flutters.

As soon as we got inside we knew that we were in the right place. Skin, hair, flesh, sweat—people moving in all directions, lights in all colors, sound surrounded us and lifted us up. Trance at last! No drugs necessary. Just a beat underneath and on top a swelling chord that builds and bends until it's about to break and gets louder and louder until it evaporates. For a split second it was silent, and I could hear the sound of the Earth turning on its axis. It was the longest second in the history of the world, like the moment before an accident or an act of violence when you have that clarity, that certainty of what's about to happen.

Instantly, the beat dropped. Sound was everywhere, and we moved so freely that our bodies became one and our minds disappeared. Cole was smiling, hair matted to his head, moisture running down his perfectly square jaw and onto his neck. I moved in all directions at once. I felt like my limbs didn't exist. I didn't exist. I felt like part of an ant colony or a beehive, or like a single atom moving fast enough to circle the Earth in eighteen seconds. The whole stadium jumped to one beat, almost as one body. I laughed hard and whirled, watching the beautiful bodies and shining eyes around us, as we were all swallowed up by the music. We were beings of pure, shimmering adrenaline.

And then, somehow I felt everything I had been ignoring and swallowing and pushing down for months. I was angry and happy and wrecked with despair. I felt like I might cry from how beautiful it all was, and I felt like I could leap a million miles into the air. This was my body. Doing exactly what I wanted it to. Nothing that had happened before was ever going to hold me down. *Nothing* would keep me here. *Nobody* would tell me what to do with my body or my mind again. Ever.

I smiled at a girl wearing a beaded tiger mask and then she danced close and rubbed up against me. She shouted into my ear over the pulsing beat.

"What?" I shouted back, my arms around her neck.

"You're so beautiful, even under that wolf hat!" she said, then her expression changed. "Hey! You're that girl from TV, from Minnesota! They're showing pictures of you all over. Are you okay?"

I stopped moving and stared at her. She was high on MDMA. I looked around for a moment and realized how many people had their phones out, filming and taking pictures. Suddenly I was afraid they'd take a picture with me in it and we'd be found out.

I looked around for Cole but couldn't see him. I wanted to grab him and slip into the crowd, get lost.

I told the girl I didn't know what she was talking about and that I was from California, just there with my boyfriend, didn't know anything about some kids from Minnesota. I surveyed the crowd again for Cole, trying to keep my sense of panic at bay. Maybe someone recognized him and called security or the cops. How did I lose him so quickly? What if he had taken off and left me there dancing? What if I had to go back to Minneapolis alone?

"You sure you're okay?" the girl asked. "Oh! Is it a bad trip? You want some water?" She handed me the plastic bottle she was holding. I pushed past her through the crowd. I heard someone calling my name and ran faster toward the exit. Now the music was a frantic soundtrack for my anxiety. I started running, but a hand caught my arm and jerked me back.

I made a fist and turned, ready to swing, but it was Cole: sweat covered, flushed, his eyes dark with excitement and sorrow.

"Are you trying to leave me?" he shouted.

I put my arms around him and we held each other, our hearts beating fast against each other's chest.

"What's going on?" he said into my ear.

"Everyone can recognize us."

He said, "Then we have nothing to lose."

"We do. They'll catch us and take us back home!"

I looked up and kissed him, tasted the saltiness of his skin.

"Not without a fight," he said.

We moved through the crowd, freer than ever. Then ran along the asphalt outside the gate.

6/8, AFTER MIDNIGHT

A new day!

From up here, I can see galaxies and constellations of living, breathing stars in the form of people packed together in a nuclear cluster in the middle of the Nevada desert. I'm sitting on top of this insane Ferris wheel, looking down on a reflection of the night sky made of teeming humanity, lights flashing in the distance. It looks like some crazy scene out of a sci-fi film, like an alien ship has landed, or maybe we're the alien ship. And I can see glittery confetti falling down and rising up over the crowd in the distance, all lit up in blue and silver. And Tycho is playing, and I just want to stay here and watch and I also want to go back in and dance, and I want to get back on a fast ride all at the same time.

In the distance, projected on a fluttering silver screen, scenes from down below make it look like the crowd extends everywhere, and I can't tell who is real and who is video, who is projection. Lisette would *love* this.

I have never been to an amusement park, even the one in the Mall of America, and this is the king of all amusement parks. We went on something that spun so fast it held us in place with centrifugal force. So. Much. Fun. It finally feels like enough is going on, like when I was a kid and would study with the TV on and the neighbors' music through the wall and my own music going too. Reading, thinking, watching, listening—doing everything at once.

Cole and I rocked back in our seat and looked up into the hazy, light-polluted sky, blue flashes from the laser show like lightning playing across the misty gray expanse. Only the moon was visible, so we howled at it.

I was sad that I had to lose my halo of white hair to make the trip—but I love being in disguise up here in the middle of nowhere, wearing Lisette's hat. If only we could go higher.

6/7, EVEN LATER

S eeing stars!

Rushed and pushed through with the crowd and then I am actually about to faint because I recognize the beat immediately and it's Deadmau5 playing. Like something in a dream, and we're laughing and then pushing farther in. The sound feels like it's coming from inside my body it's so intense, my chest beating like a drum, and for a minute I wish I'd brought earplugs and I can't hear Cole and we are screaming at each other, laughing, and then jumping, jumping all in unison with the crowd, arms raised, kandi (EDM speak for bracelets) flashing. Up on the screen behind Deadmau5—his enormous image projected, the big, round, cartoonish robot mouse head. Heat and sweat and bodies everywhere. Mouths moving, singing along. Skinny geeky kids like us, glitter-buttered pixies and muscled Festival Bros. Everyone is singing:

It's been so far, I've been walking the line on my own,
lift me up to the stars, we are coming home.

Cole's eyes are brilliant blue. He's got his hands on my hips, and we're dancing, his face raised, awash in flickering light. And we are millions of light-years away from where we came from. Minneapolis skyline; the roof of our building; the cramped, empty apartment Cole shared with his mother; the hiding out at Rita's just to get time alone. We've given everything up: the accident, the fight, the missed court appearance, the names my father called him, taking care of Jennifer, that terrible Christian retreat, and those coarse hands on my body. All washed away, sonically obliterated. I feel breathless and free in a way I never dreamed possible. A way I will never give up.

6/7, LATE

Twenty-one hours of driving, three hours of sleep, sixteen hundred miles. Tired. Wired. The longest day I've ever lived. Every nerve raw.

When Cole saw the turnoff he got so excited that I thought he'd drive us right into the ditch! He had a look of joy on his face that I hadn't seen in a month, his eyes shone and his thin lips curled into a gentle smile. The Las Vegas Speedway! Home to the Electric Daisy Carnival—EDC! Electronic dance music's mecca—hundreds of thousands of people jumping to the beat, sweating, screaming, living. Neon lights, massive glowing mushrooms, an owl four stories high. As we got to the top of the off-ramp we caught a glimpse of the whole thing and we both gasped. Fireworks exploded directly above us, sending stars shooting in every direction. Beyond the endless parking lot, a ring of red, orange, and purple light. I thought of Rita and the way that she loved all things purple. Loved a party. She would have been amazed to see this place. I wish we could have brought her with us. The woman who taught Cole to dance.

No one would find us in a crowd like this! We could disappear and be exactly where we always wanted to be at the same time. It was almost midnight, but the music would be playing until six a.m. and the parking lot was a sea of cars. We found a spot about a million miles from the speedway and squeezed in the little Prius.

From the parking lot we could see inside the ring of light. A whole galaxy of waving arms, moving shoulders, heads bouncing. The music pulsed, and the car hummed. For a moment, it felt like the world had stopped spinning.

"Hey, kids!" The impossibly high voice was attached to a short girl with white lipstick and a stadium-size smile. She wore bright-blue furry boots that would have made our friend Lisette swoon, a dark-blue-sequined bikini, and gold-sequined ribbon wrapped around each of her legs. Her arms were covered with beaded kandi bracelets from wrist to elbow, and on her head was a huge gold bow. Her smooth bronzed skin sparkled in the stadium lights.

"Looks like we're all a little late to the party, huh?" she said.

"Looks like we're just in time to me!" I said, and nearly tripped over myself getting out of the car. "And we don't even know how we're going to get in."

"Aww, let's find you some tickets, sister!" She bounced

off toward the lights, and we followed behind her feeling lighter than air. As we walked, Cole and I took stock of what we had: six hundred and forty dollars that we took from Rita's apartment (probably her life's savings), six packages of beef jerky, and this journal. In the fancy eco-correct car we'd stolen from yoga-lady we had the pencil box, my telescope, and a backpack with some clothes.

After all that we'd been through in the last three days, we were looking pretty ragged and ready for a rave. My head was shaved down to a fine layer of bleached hair, my mascara smudged, and I had all my kandi from Lisette. I changed out of that ridiculous flowery-print dress (my undercover-as-college-student look) into a T-shirt with a drawing of an atom on it and some black shorts that were in my bag. I was still getting used to Cole's short hair; he looked like a different person with those Wayfarer sunglasses we picked up in the thrift store. He was wearing ripped-up jeans and had taken off his shirt. His smooth broad chest gleamed under the halogen lights, and he wore his glow-in-the-dark bracelets.

In the shadow of the bleachers, Cole stopped to talk with a huge pink-fleshed man wearing a bright-yellow bandanna, wraparound sunglasses, and a cutoff T-shirt that read BLURNT. A minute later we had our day passes and five hundred dollars still in our pockets.

"The guy wanted to throw in a parachute of Molly, but I

told him that we just like to dance," Cole said.

We walked toward the entrance, high on adrenaline and the realization that we were actually here. Then I stopped. Outside the speedway was a cluster of cops. Would they recognize us? I was ready to run back to the car at the other end of the lot. Get out of here as quickly as we could. Cole felt it. He took my hand and leaned in close to me. "They're not thinking about us."

At the gate, a thick-necked guard looked at our tickets, patted us down, and confiscated our beef jerky.

6/7, DOZING, DREAMING

Dream:

The same one. The one I don't want to have. In the woods.
I hate the woods. The stars are bright. I have my binoculars.
He says he has to go back to his cabin, will I come with him?
And I say yes. I say yes. I have to check your breathing, he
says. It's not a religion, it's a relationship. His big white face
in front of me. Cheeks red from the cold, a web of burst
capillaries. The sticky-sweet smell of burnt marshmallows.

Memory:

It was a few months ago; the beginning of spring—which in
Minnesota looks a lot like winter in most normal places—
and I was sitting in the physics lab after school, waiting for
the other three kids from the astronomy club to show up.
The club wasn't what you would call popular. I was watching Ms. Spencer grade lab reports and wondering what her

life was like. What does she do when she goes home? Does she watch TV and send text messages to her friends? Does she have friends? A boyfriend? In my head, I was almost fully convinced that she must be writing sci-fi novels under a pseudonym, when she looked up at me—as if she knew my thoughts.

"What's on your mind, Atty?" she asked.

I was surprised, but I didn't miss a beat. "Are you actually Maria Headley?"

She laughed. "The writer? If I were on the best-seller list, would I be teaching high school?"

"So it's not someone on the best-seller list," I said. "But you don't deny you're secretly a science fiction writer."

She shook her head and smiled at me.

"Do you know Samuel Delany?" I asked.

"You mean Chip?"

My jaw dropped, and she actually pointed at me and then started laughing.

I love Ms. Spencer. She might not be who she seems to be, but in a good way.

Fact:

The Earth spins at one thousand miles an hour, and it travels through space at sixty-seven thousand miles an hour. There are times when I feel this velocity.

6/7, NIGHT

I was sitting in the parked car trying to find something on the radio that wasn't some jerk whining about his love life when Cole came bursting out of the mini-mart. "Drive! Drive!" he called in a weird stage whisper. I slid over the shifter and put the little half-electric tin can into gear, wondering what the hell was going on.

"Oh, Atty!" He breathed. "That was close."

He pulled up his shirt and, like, fifteen packages of beef jerky fell out. He was laughing as he read off all the flavors—original, teriyaki, garlic chili, black pepper, smoked hickory, and something called kung pao (his favorite!).

"No way I was going to pay for this crap," he said, grinning in that way that I love. I smiled, felt warm and alive.

I looked in the rearview mirror and shuddered. Is this how it ends? Shoplifting snacks from a gas station in East Nowheresville, Wyoming? I glanced at Cole, then back in the mirror. But behind us, everything stayed dark.

Down I-25 to Cheyenne, west on I-80. Laramie. Fort Steele. Point of Rocks. Little America. "As if the big one weren't enough," Cole said.

Momentarily lost in some awful suburban beltway, we caught a glimpse of the moon reflecting off the Great Salt Lake and headed south. At a truck stop called Love's we ate chicken and biscuits.

After a little while it looked like everyone was staring at us.

This isn't all that unusual. Brown girl, white boy: people from the middle of nowhere don't see people like us together a lot—and there are always idiots and bigots who want to judge you with their eyes, but something seemed different about it. Like they recognized us, were trying to figure out where they knew us from.

We kept quiet and ate, leaning back in the booth to relax, looking up at the TV. Something wrong in the Middle East. Suspected terrorists arrested in Chicago. Another dumb politician making another dumb speech. And then a news conference in Minneapolis—we looked at each other. I could feel the hair on my neck rising, my heart racing in my chest. I started to get up to leave, but Cole put his hand on mine. Telling me without words to keep cool.

Next: My dad's boss on the television making a statement. Saying that kidnapping could not be ruled out. And then our pictures flashed on the screen. Fortunately, they were from when we had all our hair. Unfortunately, the chief of police said we'd probably altered our appearances. I couldn't believe what I was hearing. The story they were telling the whole world about me and Cole was a total lie.

I watched our waitress from a distance as she headed quickly to the kitchen, and I had a vision of her calling nine-one-one once she was behind the swinging doors.

We got up. Left money on the table and walked as quickly and as inconspicuously as possible (after a roomful of people just saw a televised police conference about us) out the door. We jumped in the car and sped away, my heart in my throat as Cole drove.

Mona. Nephi. Scipio. So far no one behind us. Utah is nowhere: hopefully it's nowhere enough. Dirt field after dirt field. Mountains watched us silently from the background as we headed toward Nevada.

On the road ahead, one tiny pair of headlights broke through the darkness and advanced toward us. We watched without a sound. My head felt lighter than air, and I gripped the side of my seat to keep my hand steady while Cole drove at exactly the speed limit, his eyes fixed straight ahead, his lips set tight. The oncoming car got closer and brighter, then suddenly a swirling fury of blue and white spinning lights erupted from the middle of the road between us.

"Holy shit!" Cole shouted. The flashing lights reflected off every surface inside the car and seemed to surround us from all directions at once. Red taillights came on, and a siren broke into the silence of the night.

I was too scared to talk or even move.

The police car burst into motion a few hundred feet ahead of us, made a sharp U-turn from the grassy median, and fell in line behind the car on the other side of the road.

We held our breath as the two slowed down and pulled over on the opposite shoulder. We drove past them without blinking until the lights faded and we were surrounded again by the darkness.

For a long time, neither one of us spoke. Then Cole broke the silence.

"Kidnapping?" he said. "*Kidnapping*? On top of everything else they're going to say I stole you? Troubled Minnesota youth steals car and takes his girlfriend hostage? I can't even. I'm a fugitive? I'm wanted for assault and battery? This is . . . I just can't."

"They won't win," I said. "They can tell all the lies in the world and they can turn a blind eye to the real criminals, but they can't win. We'll get where we need to go. We'll get rid of this car and find another one."

Nothing was going to stop us. Nothing.

6/7, EVENING

Writing from the passenger seat. Too nervous to sleep, and even though we're doing seventy-five on the interstate, it's more like we're crawling across the unending blankness of twilight prairies.

Dream:
I'm driving at night in a car that is made out of glass. I can see all the parts of the engine in front of me. The road is slick with lake water, and there are small fish swimming in the puddles. One jumps up and bounces off the windshield. It makes a hairline crack that grows until the entire car looks like an intricate spiderweb. Small shards begin to pierce my skin, fall into my eyes, stick in my hair. I know that I am being followed, and when I reach out for the steering wheel, it's gone.

Memory:

I went into Ms. Spencer's lab and Cole was already there.

"Atty," she said, "you're just in time."

Cole looked up from drawing a map of the circumpolar constellations and gave a quick smile. I could feel my insides melting when I looked at the angles of his jaw, the breadth of his shoulders. There was a mischievous glint in his eye.

"That's exactly what we've been talking about," he said.

Huh? I was really confused. They had been reading my mind and talking about how cute Cole is? I must have made a crazy face, because they both burst out laughing.

"Time," Cole said. "Ms. Spencer said that time has to have an arrow to exist. You know, it can only go in one direction—or else it's not time. An egg can be cracked and the insides can fall out, but it can never happen the other way around."

I thought about it.

I know about entropy, the second law of thermodynamics: Everything heads toward disintegration—chaos, if left alone. But what if things were different? What if the world had been born in another way? There's no rule of physics that says the world as we know it is how it has to be.

"Just because time's arrow only goes in one direction as the universe is *now*," I said, "doesn't mean that it couldn't have been different. If the big bang had happened differently, we could be making whole eggs from scrambled ones every morning, right?"

Cole pushed a long blond lock of hair away from his forehead and looked at me with a new expression. His mouth opened the tiniest bit, and his pale eyes felt like they were seeing deep inside of me.

"Exactly."

Fact:
An object in motion experiences time at a slower rate than one at rest.

6/7, AFTERNOON

The names all read like poetry.

Owatonna. Albert Lea. Blue Earth. Sioux Falls. The flat, dry land looks scorched and brown from the summer heat. The edge of every town is identical: car dealers, strip malls, parking lots. Houses built too close to the interstate.

We drove slowly through the blank boring neighborhoods of a town whose name we didn't know. A place as vacant as if a neutron bomb had landed, killed all the people, and left the buildings standing.

The morning sun was blazing, blinding us as we turned a corner, when Cole leaned over and asked me to pull to the curb. "Right there, by the Goodwill." He pointed. "My look needs some serious help." A short, wrinkled woman was unlocking the store as we got out of the car. She was wearing shiny black slacks and a black rayon blouse covered in tiny white printed leaves. Up close, I was surprised by the thickness of the old woman's dark-gray hair and the sureness of her hands as she turned the key in the lock. Inside, dust glittered in the bright window, and it smelled vaguely like Ms. Spencer's storage room between the chemistry and physics labs. Shirts organized by color made a dull rainbow, and for a second I thought I'd puke.

"How about this?" The Hawaiian shirt Cole was wearing had a pattern of blue mountains covered in yellow pineapples and ukulclcs on a background of bright-red swirling waves.

"Aaah!" I screamed, then burst out laughing. "Hideous!" An involuntary snort came from my face. He looked at me dubiously over a pair of scratched-up knockoff Ray-Bans. A camouflage baseball cap completed the ensemble.

"You are just about the cutest thing ever!" I wanted to push him into the fitting room and have my way with him. "But I wouldn't exactly call it inconspicuous."

"What do you mean? I'm practically invisible!" The hint of a smile tickled his lips.

"Here, try this." I handed him a pair of long khaki shorts and a totally harmless light-blue plaid casual dress shirt.

"Yeah, right. Incognito." He pretended to sulk. "Ugh. If I'm going to look like a total douche canoe, at least I can keep the sunglasses."

We paid for the clothes and got back out on the road—Reliance. Presho. Murdo. Kadoka. Dakota goes on and on, but at the edge of the Badlands I pointed us south. We drove euphoric in our getaway car. Long Valley. Swett. Porcupine. Wounded Knee. Pine Ridge; I wondered if my mother had traveled to these places. Do I have family there? Did my ancestors pass through as they were driven ever farther north? Mama says that Crazy Horse is buried near there, but no one knows exactly where. He didn't want anyone to have the satisfaction of capturing his dead heart or his bones.

Afternoon wore on as I sped across Nebraska on the two-lane road named after him and tried to escape as fast as I could.

Dream:

I am flying above the Earth, beyond the bubble of atmosphere, but breathing is easy. I look out and see the planets arranged in their places as they are in the posters on Cole's wall. In the center the massive sun is boiling. I float toward the sun, and it warms me but does not burn. Soon it's all that I can see. Orange, red, black spots exploding, and I'm swimming in the liquid heat. Disintegrating, feeling myself dissolve, drift, float like ashes.

Memory:

That day I met my grandfather, the first and last day I would know him, I expected that he would tell me some special story. I thought he would be wise and know some tale about the tribe or about native history, that he'd talk about the spirits of animals like native people do on TV. None of that happened. But after my mother and her sisters were done sitting in the living room with him, waiting, expecting something but saying nothing, they finally went into the kitchen to be with my grandmother and drink coffee. And then it kind of happened.

"You like Mickey Mouse?" he asked me.

"Uh . . . no."

"That's good," he said. "The guy who thought him up hated women."

"How do you know?"

"Look at the stupid things that mouse does."

"I've never seen it." I shrugged.

"Good," he said again.

Fact:

In twelve thousand years there will be a new North Star.

6/7, MIDDAY

So close. So terrifyingly close. It took half an hour for me to stop shaking and be able to write this. We almost didn't get out. We'd been driving for a while when we thought better about the dog walker. I wanted to keep going, but Cole insisted we take the next exit.

"We need to dump this car," said Cole. "When your dad realizes that you're gone, our faces are going to be plastered all over the news, and if that guy on Rita's block puts two and two together, every highway cop in the Midwest will have a description of a bright-purple Saturn that was hot-wired by two teenagers looking like extras from *Blade Runner*." He pulled off the interstate into a bland, flat strip mall.

I knew that we had to act and that we didn't have much time. While he was talking I was watching everyone in the parking lot, so paranoid. I surveyed everyone who went by, trying to think of something we could do to hide, or hitch a ride, or stow away somehow. Then, at the curb, a blond woman wearing a monstrous red floppy hat and a tank top was unpacking a towheaded toddler from a black Prius and heading into Office Max. I watched. She was talking on the phone, and the kid was waddling along a few steps behind, sucking on a ring of car keys. I got out of the car as calmly as I could. "I know what to do," I told Cole.

"Hey there, little man," I said to the boy, squatting down next to him on the sidewalk. His face was doughy and blank with little blue eyes like M&M's stuck in white cake icing. "Whatcha got there?" He held out the key ring to show me. "Ooh, nice, can I take a look?" The mom was walking through the automatic doors, still talking on the phone about yesterday's yoga class and paying no attention to the kid when he handed me the ring. I slipped the car remote off and handed it back to him.

"Oh yeah. Ver-r-ry cool," I sang to him, and stood aside as he followed his mother inside.

Cole grabbed the telescope and our backpacks from Rita's Saturn as I jumped into the driver's seat of the Toyota. I smiled and got back on the interstate.

6/7, EARLY MORNING

We're gone! Left that place behind. Almost gone for real. And I'm never heading back there. No way. Especially now.

I'm sitting in the passenger seat watching the early-morning sun light up Cole's face as the last bits of Lakeville and Hazelwood and all the other Minneapolis suburbs slip past. The world rushes by, and I feel like I can think better, faster than usual. My head is filled with ideas. I'm thinking about Rita and how matter can never be destroyed, and how in the seconds after the big bang the universe was the size of a pea. I'm thinking about the cells in my body, the streams of blood flowing through my veins. Sometimes I feel like I am floating above the car, that I can look down and see us: two people wrecked by the world but finally winning. See us from far away, eating snacks from the 7-Eleven, changing the music, singing loudly side by side, gazing out the window, staring blankly sometimes at the road, sometimes at each other. I haven't slept for two days.

"Now it's for real," Cole said. "No one will ever keep us apart."

6/7, DAWN

Sitting in the front of Rita's old Saturn. "Little Red Corvette" is coming from the dashboard, and I'm bouncing back and forth between elated, terrified, ecstatic, and deeply sad. A dirty tissue crumpled in the ashtray has her lipstick smeared on it, and I can smell Rita's scent all around.

Today started early. We met in the stairway when it was still dark. Cole touched my arm with one finger, and I felt an electrical current complete a circuit running around the entire Earth. This is right, I thought. This is good.

We made our way through the silent streets to Rita's house on South Harriet and went around to the side. The edge of the sky was just starting to gray as the Earth turned itself toward the sun, but already the day was gross. My armpits were sweating, and my shirt was starting to stick to my back. Cole took the spare key from its usual spot—the backside of an owl sculpture made of driftwood, old cans, and wire—and opened the door. Inside, it was hard not to feel awful. The house still smelled alive, looked like someone would be home soon. I almost thought I could smell the rich, sweet smell of Rita's cooking. But it was horrifyingly empty. I could see the stunned grief on Cole's face, his eyes filling with tears. Everything we were doing seemed crazy. But then I thought of Rita and how she wanted us to be together, how she told us to do what we wanted, not to listen to other people.

My resolve to go on with our plan returned, until I caught a glimpse of myself in the mirror and suddenly felt doomed.

I said, "A short black girl with silver hair and plastic bracelets and a tall, blond, shaggy-haired white boy! Cole, we will be so easy to find."

"I don't think I can get any shorter or darker," he said.

"Come on. Let's see what's in the bathroom cupboard."

Cole raised his eyebrows and looked at me sideways.

I almost laughed. "Not *that*, you idiot."

I hopped in front of him and pulled his forehead down against mine. His smell was intoxicating, made me think of fresh earth and sweet milky tea. Heat radiated from his body. Cole looked into my eyes and said, "Atty Taton, you are the best thing that ever happened to me."

I touched his face and kissed his cheek, then took his hand as we headed up through the empty house, past Rita's tapestries, her paintings along the stairwell. Landscapes, winter scenes, birds.

I rummaged around through boxes of hair bands and jewelry. The cupboard was filled with a weird variety of things: makeup and lotions, a headless doll, an inflatable pillow, a toy boat, paintbrushes, a book of poetry by e. e. cummings. Finally I found what I was looking for: an electric hair clipper and a pair of barber's shears. I have no idea why she had them, but with Rita you never really asked why.

When we finished, I was pretty proud of my work. Cole looked like an average guy. And my hair was shorn so close you could barely make out the silver Manic Panic. Short and chic. Well, almost bald, but better than nothing.

A 1980s-looking sleeveless blue-and-white flowery dress from Rita's closet that read *Laura Ashley* on the label completed my transformation from a wild-haired EDM raver to a close-cropped, earnest college freshman studying postcolonial literature and feminist theory at UC Berkeley. It was the first time I'd heard Cole laugh in days. He stopped when he looked at himself in the mirror, though. For a minute I thought he was going to break down again.

Cole's crew cut was shocking; as though beneath his nerdy raver exterior there lurked some bro on his way to the yacht club. We'd have to stop and pick up a preppy outfit for him once we got out on the road.

We'd taken a wad of twenty-dollar bills from the dresser and some of Rita's cassette tapes. But the little Chinese bowl on the windowsill that usually held her keys and paper clips only had paper clips in it. And then Cole did kind of lose it.

"Shit." He put his hands on his head, walked away from me, and stood for too long in the living room. The room that was completely full of all her paintings. I could hear him crying softly.

"I'm sorry," he whispered, and threw himself down on the couch.

"It wasn't your fault," I said. "It was an accident. But, Cole, we have to go *now* or it will be much worse."

I wanted to comfort him to take away all he had been through. And for a moment I thought we should abandon the plan altogether. I thought maybe we should go talk to someone. Maybe we should talk to my parents or Ms. Spencer or someone, tell them how it really was. Tell them we needed help. But every time I imagined how we would actually do it, I thought of my mother saying that I should go to church and confess my transgressions. And I knew we were doing the right thing.

"Listen, we have to figure out how to get out of here! We can't leave without a car," I said. "Hitchhiking is too risky; someone will recognize us even like this."

"No," he said, wiping his eyes, taking a shuddering breath. Then he looked at me and actually smiled. He was so used to grief, living day to day with it. Surviving.

"We're going to get out of here, Atty. I know what to do."

He said it with such confidence that I didn't ask questions, just followed him through the door and out onto the sidewalk. The old purple Saturn was parked right in front.

Silently, Cole opened the passenger door, leaned inside, and reached around under the dashboard for a few minutes. The hood popped up slightly, and he went around to open it all the way.

Out of the corner of my eye, I could see a round, pasty-gray bald man wearing checkered shorts and a blue oxford coming down the block. He was walking a sickly little dog. I could feel the blood pumping through every vein in my body. What if he knew Rita? What if he knew what had happened to her?

"Morning!" the man said.

"Morning," Cole answered, sticking his head out from behind the open hood. "Sure looks to be a hot one today."

"Car troubles, eh?"

"Oh, yeah. It's always one thing or another with this old clunker," Cole replied.

"Ah. It's a good thing that you're handy," he said as he walked away. "Keep cool."

Cole nodded, gently closed the hood, got in the driver's seat, and started the car. I got in with my heart swelling and looked at Cole. "Where did you learn that?"

He said a word I'd never heard him use.

"Mom."

6/7, NIGHT

Busted.

Lisette's pain-in-the-ass racist mother must have called and snitched to my parents. I should go over there and smother that woman in her sleep! I want to punch out the windows in my room. I have to tell myself to keep calm. Stay cool. Think this all through. We'll stick to the plan. Get away.

It's about two a.m. now and I'm under the covers with my penlight, just like up at the church retreat, and the feeling of it is making me sick. I can't sleep. In a couple of hours I'll sneak out, meet Cole in the stairway, and we'll be gone for good. We'll have to get out of town quickly, because when Papa wakes up for work and finds me gone there won't be a minute to spare.

This evening, after Cole and I made our decision to run away, I went over to Lisette's to say good-bye. We sat in her room, and she cried. I cried too, but only for a minute.

"Promise me you'll come back," she pleaded.

"I'll come back," I lied.

I told her that we didn't know where we were going or how we'd get there—another lie. We talked about all the things we'd done together, and she told me she wanted to come with us. When I told her no, she looked angry, then sad, then relieved. She threw her arms around me.

I thought I heard her mother outside the door, but we had put a Diplo album on so no one could hear us talking, and it made it hard to be sure. I shouldn't have told Lisette in the first place.

Lisette dug around under the bed and handed me her wolf hat.

"In case you need a disguise," she said, wiping her face.

When I got home Papa was waiting for me.

"Atabei, *ti chouchou*, your mother and I, we love you so much. These days have been very difficult, but you must stay with us. You must trust us. We know how hard it is, but running away is not how to solve any problems. It never works, *ti chouchou*. Never."

Said the man who left Haiti because it was violent and crazy and there was nothing there for him. Says the man who met his wife at a Prince concert.

My mother said she had been praying for me to come to my senses.

Thanks!

I lied to them too. I told them I was just frustrated and sad and I would never really run away, especially with school and finding out about the National Merit Scholarship. I said I knew how they felt about Cole, and that they needed to trust me that he was a good person, but that I would obey them and not see him anymore.

"Of course he's a good person," my mother said. And I watched my father scowl as she did; he won't let up for a minute.

"I pray for Cole and his family every day," my mother said. "But you can't save him, Atty, he has to come to Jesus. He has to pay for the things he's done."

It is unfathomable to me that they looked relieved, looked like they believed me, when I said, "I guess you're right." I knew that they would be keeping an extra eye on me now, but I also knew that with their long shifts, their opposite schedules, one of them would have to call out of work to make sure I didn't go anywhere. Something neither of them would do. And anyway, I'm leaving sooner than they think.

There is no way I'm staying, no way I'm leaving Cole, and no way anyone is coming to Jesus.

Dear Lisette,

I'm sorry to leave without really saying good-bye. You've been my only real friend since seventh grade, and I know it's lousy of me to run off without you—but I'm sure you'll find a way to understand that what Cole and I are doing is the only choice that we have.

I don't know how I'm going to get this note to you, but it seems so shallow to send a text that just says "Bye, you're the best." And I don't think that I can explain it at all over the phone. There's nothing here anymore for me and Cole, so we're leaving and I don't think we'll be coming back.

Your very best friend,
Atty

No, that's all wrong. I've got to go see her. Tell her what's going on. She deserves a real good-bye.

6/6, LATE AFTERNOON

I'm sitting in the stairway near the fourteenth floor of our building. The days are all starting to bleed into one, but maybe I can keep my head on straight by writing it all out.

I got a text from Cole during lunch at school. He was back home!

I cut out the side door and went straight there. I guess Jennifer was out wandering the streets somewhere looking for something to sell out of the garbage, or trying to get her fix, so we were alone again at last.

Cole looked so tired and hollow, shaken. But his kiss was gentle and slow and deep. At first we didn't even speak but looked into each other's eyes, held each other on his bed. I felt the muscles in the small of his back beneath his shirt as his strong hands softly stroked my skin. It makes me lose my balance and nearly drop the pen from my hand when I think about our bodies and minds being together like that. I could hold him forever.

After, he told me everything that had happened to him since yesterday. The patrol car to the Fourth Precinct, fingerprints, photographs; the night spent in a holding tank with two winos and a dude who had punched his wife. Cole's eyes were all watery when he described how it felt to see Ms. Spencer and his mother at the station this morning.

"Ms. Spencer! She was awesome," Cole told me. "When they brought me out from the holding cell, she was talking to your father, looking real serious. But when she saw me, her whole face lit up and she hugged me. I cried right there. Jennifer sat on a chair by the wall and watched."

Ms. Spencer dropped them off at home and went back to school. Amazingly, as soon as they got into the apartment Jennifer got wrecked. His "mother." High as a kite, she turned on the TV, made popcorn, and then nodded out.

He told me, "She didn't give a shit about what happened, didn't ask about the fight, looked at me blankly when I talked about Rita. Unbelievable, even for her. No reaction, nothing! And all of it is my fault. All of it. I'm done, Atty. There's no reason to stay here. There's nothing left for me. Except you. You're all I've got."

I thought of everything that had happened in such a short period of time, it didn't seem possible. I told him that what happened to Rita wasn't his fault. What he'd done was something I'd desperately wanted to do myself. But I knew that Cole wouldn't have a chance if it went to trial.

"If they send me to jail, I don't think I could make it."

Then I said it. "Let's leave then."

For a moment, his face brightened with relief. "You want to run away together?"

"Yes," I said. "We can take Rita's car and drive west, see the EDC, then go to California. I've never seen the ocean. From there we can go to Mexico, to the observatory in Baja. San Pedro Mártir! We could actually see it. Just you and me and all the stars in the universe." I kept talking, desperate to get us out of this situation.

I gazed at Cole. His sadness sometimes felt like a weight that was pulling us both down. And sometimes the feeling of holding him up is all that keeps me going.

"Please," I said. "We've come through so much already. Let's go and never turn back."

I knew that distance didn't mean anything. There were things that made me feel hopeless like he did, and they followed me wherever I went. My whole body went momentarily numb when I thought of it. Running away might not fix it, but it would be a distraction—and certainly leaving our families behind would be better. Much better. I didn't think it could get worse.

"Yes," he said.

I kissed him, looked deep into the ocean of his eyes. The only ocean I knew.

"Yes," he said again. "I love you, Atty."

6/6, MORNING

This waiting is making me insane!

I'm in the library writing this and trying not to lose my mind over what happened yesterday. It was the first time that I'd seen that side of Cole, and it was scary. Could he ever be like that with me? He couldn't, I know he couldn't.

He was just doing something that I wished I had the strength to do, and I've imagined much worse.

I got to school half an hour early today and found Ms. Spencer in the physics lab. She was reassembling one of the gas burners, with an intense look of concentration on her face and a long yellow screwdriver in her hand. The second I saw her I totally lost it, tears streaming down my face.

"You have to help! You're the only one who can!"

I gulped in air while trying to tell her what had happened.

Ms. Spencer was wearing her "Look, I'm a scientist"

outfit—white lab coat over black jeans and a V-neck T-shirt. Her fine dark hair tied up in a knot.

Her face stayed calm as she pulled over a lab stool and sat me down. I love that woman. Handing me a wad of tissues, she said, "That's right, Atabei, get it all out. And when you're ready, tell me the whole story. From the beginning."

God, if only my parents would speak to me that way—the world would be a different place. Finally I stopped sobbing and managed to say a few coherent words.

"Cole is in jail!"

Her pale hazel eyes widened for a second, and she waited for me to go on.

"He . . . he got into a fight after school. I saw it happen. It's *my* fault really. He's been really upset since Rita's accident. I had been complaining about Daniel, and then we saw him after school, and . . ." I almost told Ms. Spencer everything, but I stopped short.

The lines in her face deepened as if she already knew my secrets, and her eyes grew two shades darker.

"Lisette tried to stop him," I went on, "but then the police came and arrested him. My father won't do anything to help, and Cole's mother is a total basket case! Ms. Spencer, you have to help him. They'll send him off to prison, I just know it."

Ms. Spencer's face reddened, then quickly returned to normal. She looked at me silently for a minute that felt like an hour.

"Okay, take a deep breath and listen to me." She put her hands on my shoulders. "I'm going down to the station right now to straighten this out. I'll pick up Jennifer and take her there. I'll talk to your father. He's at work?"

I nodded.

"You get yourself to class."

She took off her lab coat, put on her cardigan, and left as the bell rang for the start of school.

That's the last I heard—and now all I can do is wait.

6/5, NIGHT

I've never been so angry in my life. Beyond angry—furious!
Papa thinks I can't see what he's doing. He thinks I
don't know he just wants Cole to stay away from me and
will do anything he can to make that happen, even if he
abuses his power.

He told me, "Battery is a serious offense. Daniel filed
charges."

I nearly screamed at him. I couldn't believe we were even
having this conversation. "They didn't have to take him in,
and you know it!"

"They did, *ti chouchou*, it's their job."

Had to? Had to? I thought that I would strangle my
father right there. Calling me "my dear" in Creole like I'm
some little kid. So condescending and smug. I am sick of
hearing those words. I am not a child. Cole had to go to

the police station, but Lisette went home when her mother came to the scene. Her mom was furious, of course. Cursing at the cops, cursing at me. Papa got there later, it might have been five minutes or it might have been an hour. I can't tell. He sat me in the back of his patrol car until everyone else left. Then he drove me home.

Papa doesn't know anything about my life anymore, doesn't know why the fight happened. I would never tell him; he would never understand.

By the time we got home I wanted to rip the badge right off my father's jacket and throw it across the dining room. Instead, I picked up the nearest object—a framed picture of my family—and smashed it against the wall. Little bits of glass tinkled onto the floor. A ceramic figurine of Jesus pointing to his thorn-encircled heart fell off a nearby shelf, and that smashed too, and then Mama was there.

"Now you come out of your room?" I screamed at her. "*Now* you suddenly have eyes? Do you know what they did to Cole today?"

"How dare you wake your mother and talk to her like that," my father said. "You know she is working second shift. You know this is the only time she can sleep."

"Atabei, calm down," Mama said.

"No. Mama, they arrested my boyfriend. Put him in handcuffs in front of everyone."

My mother and father looked at each other.

"He assaulted Daniel, Grace. It was bad," Papa told her.

Even though Daniel deserved it, I felt so ashamed and hopeless.

"Daniel?" Mama said. "But why?"

I couldn't answer. I couldn't say it.

"I know that Cole is troubled, sweetheart. But *Daniel*? He'd never fight anyone. It makes no sense."

I stood still. Shaking. Silent.

Mama picked up the pieces of the porcelain Jesus and put them in the trash, shaking her head.

"*Ti chouchou*," Papa said. "You know how it works. He's seventeen. He will be given a court date and released as soon as someone can come claim him."

"Which you know can't happen!" I shouted. "The only person who could have done that is gone! And God knows where his mother is. He manages all by himself. He's not out on the street, he's getting the same grades as me, he does everything right, and he has no one."

"If no one can come and get him, Child Protective Services will be involved. That probably should have happened a long time ago."

I headed for the door, but my father grabbed me by the arm and pulled me back.

I wrenched myself free from his grip.

"You need to talk to the police," I said. "You need to go there and tell them everything. Tell them it's not what he's really like, he was just upset."

"People who are just upset don't try to kick a person to death," Papa said. "They could have charged him with attempted manslaughter—you don't see the favors I'm already doing for you."

"He was just upset," I said again.

Mama said, "Atabei, this is not you talking. A devil has hold of you. You will go to your room and you will stay there."

"A devil has hold of *me*?" I asked her. "You're so blind, you can't see what's happening right in front of you!"

I went to my room and slammed the door. We're sixteen floors up, so I couldn't climb out the window.

All I can see is Rita's blank face and Daniel's bloodied one. It all seems impossible. I can't imagine what Cole is going through at the police station, and I need to go to him, talk to him, hold him. How could all this have happened? It's so much that my head is spinning. I have to find someone who can post bail. But even if I do, Cole will be stuck there all night. I can't go downstairs to his apartment and talk to Jennifer, and even I know it's wrong for my parents to just shut me away in my room after something like this.

Everyone is insane.

There's only one person who can help.

As soon as I get to school I will go talk to Ms. Spencer.

6/5, AFTERNOON

So much has happened so fast! I can barely write about it. The bell rang. School ended.

Lisette said that she was dying for those french fries that come wrapped in a paper cone with twenty-seven different kinds of ketchup. I think they're nasty, but I was feeling numb and there wasn't anything else to do before the astronomy club meeting at four o'clock, so Cole and I walked with her toward Third Avenue South. We had barely walked for two minutes when I saw him out of the corner of my eye.

Across the street there was a dollar store with boxes of tissues and mops and votive candles in the window. Daniel was standing out front between two parked cars and walked out into the road toward us with a big smile on his face. I could see his wet purple-pink lips and perfectly even gleaming white teeth.

"Hello!" he called out as he crossed and waved. "Atty!"

Everything about him made me sick: His large pale forehead that shone with a film of sweat. His small gray eyes that were set too close together above his upturned nose. The dimple in his chin rubbed raw and pink from shaving.

The three of us stopped walking and waited for him to come over.

"Hi," I managed to sputter. Even though I wanted to throw up.

"Well *hello!*" he said cheerfully, glancing at Cole and Lisette. "You must be friends of Atty's. Nice to meet you."

I could feel the air change around Cole. His whole body became tense, his face turned to stone, and his light eyes turned suddenly dark. He stepped between us and looked right at Daniel.

"I think you'd better keep on moving," Cole said firmly. "We're not interested in talking to you."

"I'm just saying hello to a friend from church."

"I *said*, you'd better keep moving!" Cole's voice was rising steadily. My heart pounded in my chest.

"I'm not sure why you're so—" But Daniel didn't finish his sentence. Cole's fist hit his nose, sending a fine spray of blood all over me and Lisette, who screamed, "What the *fuck*, Cole!"

Stunned, Daniel doubled over, holding his face. Cole grabbed Daniel's head and smashed it with his knee, sending him sprawling to the ground screaming in pain.

It happened so fast! Lisette yelled "Stop!" and jumped at

Cole, who turned his shoulder and flung her into a parked car. He glared at her, then set his teeth tightly and kicked Daniel in the chest. I heard a soft cracking sound. Daniel gasped and let out a cry. Then Cole kicked him again and again. Stomach, back, legs, head.

Daniel flailed one arm wildly, and I heard him groan in a voice that I didn't want to remember. Blood stained his collar and jacket, and a million thoughts went through my mind: actual joy at seeing Daniel get what he deserved mixed with intense horror that Cole seemed capable of killing him! Cole's face had a look that I had never seen before, anger that I never knew he had.

Lisette put her head down and this time knocked Cole off-balance with a flying tackle. I heard the siren in the distance getting nearer, and two men who must have been standing nearby rushed over to where Lisette and Cole were wrestling on the ground. They grabbed Cole's arms, and one man put his knee on Cole's chest, pinning him to the ground. Lisette staggered up, while Cole kicked wildly into the air, unable to stand. Daniel lay on the ground next to him, giving off a steady low moan.

The siren blared in my ear. Two uniformed policemen rushed up just as Cole broke free of the man who held him down. He was about to kick Daniel again, but the cops grabbed him by the arms and flung him facedown on the hood of a parked car. I heard the smack of Cole's skull bouncing off the metal.

"NO!" I shouted. The sound of my own voice jolted me into motion and I threw myself onto the policeman who was holding Cole and trying to put handcuffs on him. I saw Cole's face flat against the smooth black paint of the car as the second cop pulled me off by my shoulders and turned me toward him.

"Atabei!" he shouted.

Papa? I thought. No, not Papa. A white officer. A friend who I had seen in our house and whose name I couldn't remember. He used to be Papa's partner. Then I realized—there were going to be questions. Many questions. A new terror took hold of me, and I collapsed in tears. How could I tell anyone?

I heard Daniel whimpering as he lay on the ground. Why had Cole done this? Who could explain?

I felt the expanding universe switch its course and begin to compress. It closed in on me from all sides, and I knew that my life was changed. Cole's life was changed. Our fates intertwined.

6/4, ALMOST MIDNIGHT

I looked out at the city haze and stared at the glow of the orange night sky, waiting for Cole. It seemed like a light-year passed between the time I sent him a text asking him to meet me and when I saw his shadow come through the door to the roof. I was sitting in the same place he sat the day I first found out we lived in the same building.

Cole walked straight over to me, put his arm around my waist, and kissed me.

"I came as soon as I could," he said. "Jennifer's in a mood, and she's been on my back all day about nothing but bullshit." He rolled his eyes, and I tried to smile. I guess it wasn't too convincing.

"What's going on? You look a little freaked out."

I made a lame attempt at telling him nothing's wrong; I'm just worn out and sad about Rita. But I couldn't pull it off. Finally I said, "It's a total shit show down there in my apartment."

Cole squinted his eyes slightly. Waited.

"My dad always thinks he knows what's best even when he doesn't have a clue. My mom is always going on about patience and Jesus and church! If I have to hear about how amazing Daniel is one more time, I'm going to murder someone!" I must have been yelling, because the echo of my voice came bouncing back at me from the other side of the street.

Cole said, "I don't trust that guy for a second, Atty. Gives me the creeps. Something about his eyes that I just can't figure out." Cole was quiet, thinking. I looked at him without breathing. "When you went on that retreat—to help out with the little kids—it's like a part of you didn't come back." He stared straight at me. "Atty. Did something . . . ?"

Cole's face was beautiful. Open. Loving. But I couldn't speak, or even blink.

Cole knew what it was to feel trapped and ashamed. Cole knew who I was; he respected me. He loved me.

I nodded my head, then watched his eyes dim for a second. He said, "Daniel."

Not quite a question, but his voice rose in something that sounded like pain. My pain.

I nodded again, almost. There was nothing between us now.

A cloud passed over the moon above us, making a shadow where I hadn't realized there had been light. Cole took my hand. "Oh, Atty," was all he said. He put his arms around me and held me. Gentle and strong.

6/4, NIGHT

I walked in expecting to find the apartment empty, maybe my mother in the shower getting ready for the nightshift—but when I opened the door, there's my father and mother and Daniel all standing around the dining room table. Like it's the most natural thing in the world. I thought I was going to be cool. Just walk past them. Ignore them.

"Hi, Atty," Daniel said smoothly.

As soon as I heard his voice, my stomach wrenched and my mouth filled with bile. I ran into the bathroom just in time to puke up my lunch. It happened so fast, so seemingly out of my control.

After, I felt normal. Blank. I cleaned my face, brushed my teeth, and went back to find out what was going on. "Sorry," I said, "I'm not feeling too well today." I don't know why I said that. I should have just gone to my room. I wasn't the one who should be apologizing.

My father stood up and went to the stove, put the kettle on. "You need some mint tea," he said. Because of course my father knows what everyone needs. I couldn't believe I was standing in the same room with these people. That he could come into my house and sit there with my parents. That he could sit there looking at me, my mother and father on either side.

I tried to act as calm as possible, which I did by watching the scene as if it were a stage play and I was sitting in the balcony. Mama explained that since yesterday was "so stressful," she and Papa thought it would be nice to have Daniel over for an early dinner. She said maybe doing some work at the church might make me feel better. She said I could help Daniel teach an astronomy class to the youth group once a week. He could pick me up and drop me off.

"It would really be no trouble," he said.

As they spoke, I felt my vision widening and the room compressing all at the same time. Daniel was still talking but I didn't hear any of it, and the humming in my ears got louder and louder. I grabbed my backpack with my journal, managed to mutter something about having plans with Lisette, and left.

I didn't want to hang around the elevator in case they tried to stop me—so I'm up here on the roof, writing and waiting for Cole.

6/4, DAWN

It's daybreak, and the city is quiet outside my window. Sitting up in bed. My eyes hurt. Exhausted and wide-awake at the same time. At least the writing keeps me going—well, and Cole.

Dream:
We're at the ocean. Me and Cole. Somewhere in California or Mexico. The sun is warm on our skin, and we are sleepy, listening to the waves crash. His hair is the color of sand, his eyes shiny blue in the sunlight. I can see the freckles on his shoulders. In the dream we live somewhere nearby. He says we should go back to our house. We walk along in the surf. Everywhere there is life, not the kinds of things you see at the beach. Like miniature versions of squirrels, cats, dogs, tiny polar bears, giraffes, leopards, porcupines. They are walking along the beach with us. When I look closely I

see that there is something wrong with each one—a missing foot, a bloody stump where an arm should be, a long thin gash in its back, a crushed skull. I'm terrified, and I keep thinking, We'll never fit all these things in our house.

Memory:

In sixth grade we had a project where we had pen pals with a school in New York City. Like old-fashioned pen pals where you write a letter on paper and someone writes you back. Our teacher wanted us to talk to them about what it was like in Minneapolis ("the Mini Apple," she said), and they would talk to us about what it was like in the "Big Apple." Me and the girl who was my pen pal wrote to each other about the show *Cosmos*; we didn't talk about anything that was going on where we lived, except one time she told me she took a subway train to the ocean. I didn't have anything to top that. I think I remember this so well because it was the first time I realized that I didn't have to live where I was. The first time I wanted to leave.

Fact:

Microorganisms have been brought back to life after being frozen for *three million* years.

6/3, NIGHT

It's almost midnight and I can't sleep. I'm so worried about Cole. Rita's gone! He hasn't even had time to absorb the shock. His mother is no help—doesn't care or is too screwed up to understand. My parents still won't let me see him, so we're always sneaking around.

How is any of this happening? Days ago my life was totally different. I had just seen the polar ice caps on Mars. I was worried about becoming a National Merit Scholar. Now I want to change it all back. There has to be a way. Cole and I are smart enough to figure out how to get through this. How to be together. How to have good lives, no matter what is going on around us. Or what had happened to us.

I'm afraid to sleep, afraid I'll dream. I wish we could be somewhere else. Together, just me and Cole.

6/3, EVENING

couldn't do it. I couldn't save her. No one could. A few hours ago she was alive, walking down the street with Cole. Smiling, talking, laughing. I got in a car and came home, but not Rita. Looking back now, it's like it happened in a dream.

I leaned over her face and listened, tried to feel for any movement of air that would tell me she was alive. Please! Please! I thought. Just a little breath! My mind was racing, but my body was calm. My mother is a nurse, my father is a cop—I know how to act in a crisis.

Cole stood next to me shouting her name over and over, wailing. He got down on his knees beside me in the street.

But there was nothing.

Only a widening puddle of blood beneath her head darkening the black tar, her elbow twisted up over her shoulder, the palm of her hand all wrong and facing up. Plastic beads from the bracelets I had made for her lay scattered in the road where all traffic had stopped.

I pushed on her chest with all my weight, fist beneath my open hand. Hard! Fast! If I could get her heart to pump, there would still be hope when the ambulance came! I counted thirty times and tilted her head back, held her nose, blew into her mouth. Come on, lungs, I thought, just a little air!

Again! Again! I listened. Nothing.

Rita was dead.

I'm reading the words I've written and I can't believe it. But it's true. I saw.

Cole lay down on the hot street, faceup next to Rita. His mouth was twisted and his face grew red and wet as he sobbed uncontrollably, gasping for breath. Rita's blood stained the shoulder of his shirt. He pressed the palms of his hands into his eyes, elbows to the sky.

Two EMTs jumped out of an ambulance and ran over. The flashing lights were blinding, even in the middle of the day.

"Are you hurt?" A short man with dark hair and round glasses stood above me. I could see the smooth hair on his arms below his shirtsleeves.

I shook my head and stood up as a blond woman dressed in an identical blue-and-white uniform bent down to feel for Rita's pulse. The first medic began asking Cole questions and checking him for wounds.

Everything I'd been holding in came rushing up through my body. I turned away and threw up onto the blacktop, covering the double yellow line with bits of food and bile.

"Atty!" I looked up and there was Papa, wearing his uniform. "*Ti chouchou*, what happened?"

I pointed at Rita. "She's dead!"

Papa put his arm around my shoulders and tried to lead me to the patrol car, but I ducked down and ran to Cole, still lying on the ground with his hands on his eyes, rocking from side to side. I got down on the ground and put my shoulder on his chest, squeezed him tight. I could feel him shaking, sucking in air, pushing it out through the sobs. I knew he wasn't hurt. I saw it happen.

I had been on the bus on my way to meet them, writing in this journal, looking out the window, smiling, thinking about Cole—the way that he talks with me, listens to me, sparkles his eyes at me. I tried not to think about the youth retreat, but I couldn't keep my mind from wandering there, and it left a sour taste in my mouth. I thought about Rita and the painting she would make. My portrait. How would it turn out? What would it reveal that I couldn't see? Would it be one of those pictures that you can't walk past but have to stop and stare at? Now I'll never know.

I must have been daydreaming like that for a while, because before I knew it, the bus was sitting in traffic half a block from Hennepin and Lake Street where we'd meet. I looked up and saw Rita and Cole at the corner, and I could feel my face stretch out in an even wider smile as I took them in. Cole was wearing loose denim pants and a pale collared shirt that flapped in the breeze, the top three buttons were undone, and I could taste his skin on my lips just from seeing the hint of his chest. On his wrists were the neon bracelets that he wore the day we first met. Rita was two steps ahead of him, as usual, crossing the street and walking with purpose. She wore a dark-purple sun-dress, almost black, with small white dots that waved as she walked, and her favorite clomping-around-town shoes—black leather clogs with a tall sole that made her bounce even higher when she moved. Her salt-and-pepper hair was tied back behind her neck. I could see her strong chin and sharp cheeks in the sunlight, but her bright blue eyes were hiding behind dark round glasses. Her wrists were covered in bangles and beads, some precious, some simply pretty. She carried a brown paper shopping bag—probably some weird fabric or an ancient tool, or maybe just some apples inside, I thought.

In a second, everything changed.

A white compact car came around the corner fast—too fast! Cole's face twisted as he realized what was happening, but his scream was drowned out by the squeal of brakes and tire rubber skidding on the pavement as the front headlight slammed into Rita's hip and sent her hurtling out into the road. She landed with a horrific thud and bounced once, rolled over, and lay stretched out on her back, perfectly still.

I heard the sound of my own scream and the gasp of the other passengers. Everyone began talking at once. Then I was at the door, banging with my fists. "Let me out! Let me out!" I shouted over and over until the dazed bus driver released the doors and I ran into the road. I tripped over Rita's black clog that had flown off her foot, little colored pieces of plastic rolled in all directions.

The paramedics put Rita into a long white-nylon bag. Loaded her onto a gurney. Put her in the ambulance. Closed the swinging doors. I was still holding Cole when he stopped sobbing. He looked at me, then at the spot where Rita had been lying on the ground.

"No!" he shouted.

Cole pushed me off of him and jumped up. "No!" He punched the steel ambulance door with his fist, making a dull thump. "No!"

A blur of blue uniforms and two cops were holding him, one on each arm, as Cole struggled, kicking at the ambulance, trying to break free as they dragged him away and pushed him into the backseat of a police cruiser.

"Cole!" I screamed. I ran, but my path was blocked by another blue uniform, and then my father was holding me, his arms around me.

"It's going to be okay, my love," he said.

But he's wrong. About so many things, it's not even funny.

6/3, AFTERNOON

I'm sitting on the bus on my way to meet Cole and Rita. The sun is bright through the window, and the sky is dotted with small puffy clouds.

Lisette says I'm spending all my time with Cole and that he has stolen me away like he promised her he wouldn't. I thought about it and asked her to come with us, because I was planning on meeting Cole and Rita downtown and then going back to her house. Rita wants me to sit for a painting she's making. I told Lisette it would be cool if she came and Rita could paint both of us.

"Why would she want to?" Lisette asked.

"'Cause we're like royalty. We're like EDM queens," I told her.

"In our own minds," she said, doing that thing where she makes her eyes look crazy. She smiled her big, straight-toothed, I-just-got-my-braces-off smile. "Let me text my mom."

Of course I don't have to even write what happened next because it's so predictable.

"Goddamn it," Lisette said, throwing the phone into her backpack. "I swear to God, she tries to control every single thing that I do."

"If you get a boyfriend or girlfriend, definitely don't tell her."

"What do you mean IF?"

"When," I said. "I meant when."

Lisette is touchy on the topic of romance, which is strange. She is not in the undatable nerd category (which I was until very recently). She is funny and smart and super cool looking. She'd like everyone to think that her tastes are so particular there's no one at school she could ever be with. But we spend half our time talking about who's hot. It's almost like she has some kind of force field around her. Tall girls with a great sense of humor should attract everyone. But in Lisette's case it seems to freak them out, that and her mother. Her mother would freak anyone out.

On the way to the bus stop she asked me if I had slept with Cole. I looked at her but didn't answer, and then she said, "Oh my God! What was it like? Look at you, you can't stop smiling. Stop covering your mouth! Tell me what it was like!"

I thought of how Cole smelled, musky and sharp—slightly

sweet. How he held me as the sunlight spilled in through the windows at Rita's house. I thought of how my mind went blank and the way I could feel him everywhere, moving up from my toes, spreading into my hips, up through my back, and then a feeling of soaring. At the edge of my mind, a creeping memory from the retreat tried to push in, but I kept it out with thoughts of Cole.

"Good," I whispered to Lisette.

She waited with me until the bus arrived and then gave me a big hug.

"Nerd girl in love," she said.

6/2, NIGHT

Dream:

There is a fort made of lilac bushes, and I am standing inside. The smell of the flowers is sickening, and the sunlight comes through in patches. I feel like throwing up. In the corner of the fort, a small cardboard box sits on the dirt. I realize that inside the box is someone awful and he must stay inside the box at all costs. I pick it up and leave the fort, walking on a trail through lightly wooded hills that circle around dozens of lakes. Along the trail I meet a series of friends—I've never seen them before, but I know that they are friends of mine. We toss the box back and forth among us, kicking it and banging it, but making sure not to break it open. Eventually I get back to the fort alone. The box is gone, and I don't know where it went. Inside, it smells like the flowery perfume of lilacs.

Memory:

This was just before Mama converted. I was seven, must have been first grade. Early Saturday morning, frost over the windows where the wind bumped into the blasting radiator heat of the apartment, and for some reason Mama had the day off. We were in the kitchen. Mama was washing dishes while I cleared the table, and she turned on the old CD player that she kept by the sink. *Funk Hits of the '60s* was our favorite disc. I remember the song "Papa's Got a Brand New Bag." An old one from the time just before Mama was born. Repetitive, so catchy, with that guitar breakdown that Prince stole for "Kiss." Anyway, within about twenty seconds there was no cleaning being done, just dancing. Mama and I flailing our arms and throwing our hips around, then trying to spin in unison like we had seen the dancers do in a YouTube video from the Apollo Theater. Smiling, laughing, and probably waking up the neighbors.

Fact:

Sunspots are storms of electromagnetism that stop the movement of heat through the sun. In Europe, astronomers have been counting them daily for over three hundred years.

6/2, AFTERNOON

Rita's house is like a sanctuary. I can't believe I used to just go to school and go home and wait for my parents to be around and watch television, do homework, go to sleep. I can't believe I might never have met her. Thanks to Cole, we get to go there all the time.

At Rita's house we get treated like people. She tells us stories about when she was young and the things she did, and she doesn't try to make it some kind of stupid lesson.

The other day when I was over there she told me the story of how she fell in love with Cole's mom (they were at Macalester College in St. Paul), and how Jennifer left her for Cole's dad, who then of course left Jennifer and Cole. My parents would never talk about this kind of stuff, ever. They assume I'm too young or too stupid or too innocent to understand anything.

Cole was stretching a canvas for Rita while she and I were drinking gunpowder green tea and talking in the living room, sitting beneath her paintings of lakes and bridges and skies.

"How long were you together?" I asked Rita. I couldn't imagine anyone wanting to be with Jennifer.

She went to the shelf and got out a photo album, flipped to the front pages.

"Here," she said.

It was amazing, pictures of Rita and Jennifer when they were young—Jennifer looked so much like Cole does now it almost made me do a double take. Jennifer sitting cross-legged on a wide green lawn, her long, sand-colored hair almost down to her waist, and Rita lying with her head in Jennifer's lap. They were smiling. There was another picture of them at graduation, and then one that looked like it came from a camping trip. Jennifer looked so healthy and strong it was astounding. She was wearing shorts and hiking boots, had her hair up in a ponytail. Behind her was a thick forest.

"She wasn't always an addict," Rita said. "She had an accident, something stupid, out of the blue. A sledding accident, if you can believe it. Cole was twelve. She had a bad break, her ankle, and a compound fracture in her arm. Cole didn't have a scratch because of the way she put herself in front of him, took the impact of the tree. Jennifer got prescribed painkillers. And the rest is history. But I always suspected there was something else that made her want to shut out the world."

Cole had told me stories about his mother from before she fell apart, but seeing actual pictures and hearing it from Rita was different. I could understand why he stayed with her. Why he was dedicated to her. Like he was just not going to cause her any more pain.

Rita poured me another cup of tea.

"She's not a bad woman, Atty, though it might be hard for you to believe after the things she's done. I still love her," she said. "But I wouldn't trust her. Not anymore."

"Why didn't you get back together after Cole's dad was out of the picture?"

Rita shrugged. "I fell in love with someone else. Then someone else." She laughed. "Then with a *man*, another painter. Talented guy. Beautiful hands. He lives over on South Bryant."

"Wait, you have a *boy*friend?"

"Hell yeah, sister! Why do you think I'm gone half the time? It's not just to give you kids your privacy."

"You don't live with him?"

"It's nicer like this," she said. "People gotta have some space to breathe and sing loud off-key and pick their nose by themselves, get a good night's sleep without a body next to them. You'll see."

I could stay at Rita's all day. Sink into her couch and read something off her bookcase and think and listen to her tell stories about her life and forget about all that's happened to me. Wipe them clean from my mind. I can almost imagine telling her everything.

Rita makes you realize you can be who you want.

6/1, AFTERNOON

Sitting alone in the kitchen after school today, I thought again about my mother's family and that long walk my grandfather took.

After my grandfather told me about Mickey Mouse he fell asleep, and I went into the kitchen to listen to my mother and aunts and grandmother talk. My aunt Priscilla combed my hair until it was a big wavy halo. My grandmother said she had gotten used to being alone, but that it would be nice to have someone smart to talk to again now that her girls were all grown and out of the house. She looked over at me.

My grandmother said, "Atty takes after him, don't you think?"

Mama said, "Atty's smarter."

What did he do when he was gone? What was it that made my grandfather leave my grandmother, leave my mother and her sisters? It couldn't have been anything like what happened to me, but still I think I know how he felt. How did he do something like that and everyone welcomed him back on the reservation and never said anything about it? (Or maybe they did say things about it, but I was too young to know.)

I was thinking they must have understood that something outside of them had pushed him to do it. Maybe he'd had enough. Maybe he loved his family but he'd had enough of everything. The way everyone is pressured to act by unseen forces, by things they don't understand, by decisions made by men who supposedly speak for all of us. Or even just on a scientific level. We are all made up of things that we don't understand. Every human is host to *ten thousand* different microbe species. We are just the house they live in. And how we feel is because of how they act.

Right now I feel like taking a long walk like my grandfather did. And maybe in twenty years I can come back and sit in my living room with my parents and watch *Cosmos* and no one will say anything about how long I've been gone. Maybe I'll take a long walk to Mexico. When I come back Lisette will be a famous artist and Cole will be a famous scientist and I will just be someone who wandered.

I can picture my grandfather now and I think that whatever he did, he had to do it. It must have been an incredible release to walk away.

Dream:

I'm on the roof of our building, seventeen stories high, but it's not really our building. The architecture is shifting, and instead of the parking lot on Third Street, there is another tower exactly like ours next door. The shapes are uneven and fit together like a jigsaw puzzle. Between the two towers is a gap about six feet wide. Cole is standing on the roof of the identical tower; he looks scared and is calling out something that I can't quite hear. He wants to jump over to my side, but it's too far. I take a rope out of my schoolbag, tie it to a vent duct, and throw the other end across to him. He ties it to a pipe on his side, then looks at me, frozen. I step on the rope, and as I start to walk across, the middle of the rope goes slack and I start to fall. Suddenly I'm not on top of the building anymore, but out in the woods. I don't want to be in the woods at all. The rope is tied between an abandoned cabin and a birch sapling. And below me the forest is on fire.

Memory:

It was sometime at the end of April. I remember, because Cole hadn't moved into our building yet. The trip to the Casby Observatory was just a week or two earlier, and whenever my mind drifted, it always came back to the image of Cole looking calm and thoughtful, totally perfect.

Lisette and I walked out of school; the air felt warm and moist—spring, finally—and there were kids everywhere in little clumps: talking and joking and flirting. A girl darted in and out of the groups, chasing after a boy who had taken her backpack. I noticed Cole standing with some kids over by the strip of grass that passed for a lawn, and I steered us over that way, trying not to be too obvious about it.

"Hey!" Cole popped out from behind a monstrous ogre of a boy wearing a varsity football shirt that had a cartoon of a stinging hornet on it. Cole looked at Lisette and then right at me. "Did you hear about that new restaurant on Mars?"

"On Mars?" I squinted at him.

"Yeah, the food's really good, but there's one big problem."

"What problem is that, space boy?" Lisette was giving him attitude.

He smiled at me.

"No atmosphere!"

Fact:

The astronomer Tycho Brahe wore a fake silver nose after losing his real one in a sword fight, and he also had a pet moose that died falling down the stairs after one too many drinks. (I'm not joking. Ms. Spencer told me this last week.)

5/31

I have shortened my long list of life goals to two major points:
Win
Leave

5/30, NIGHT

Before she went to work the other day, Mama came into my room and again asked me to consider going to church to "get some guidance from the pastor." She said good grades were important but not as important as my soul. (Please.) Papa would never say my grades were not important. Because he and I know that my grades are what will get me where I need to go. Get me out of here.

Just her bringing up the church made me shut out whatever she was saying. I stared at the carpet and pretended to listen to her. The idea of even entering that place turns everything around me blank and mute. Like watching television with the sound off. I was angry, but that had to stay somewhere deep down because there was no yelling without crying, and there was no crying without explaining what I was crying about—and that is something I couldn't do.

When Mama started talking about Cole I started listening again.

I get mad at her, but Mama is always kind. Especially now that she's been born again. And she had kind things to say about Cole. She didn't think like Papa did that I should never see him again. She said she was praying for him and for his mother, and that there is always hope. And that Jesus had already found Cole, and it was now up to Cole to accept him into his heart.

She said, "Love is a powerful thing, Atty. Especially for a boy who doesn't get much of it."

5/29, FIFTH PERIOD

I saw Cole in the hallway just before the bell rang for history class. He's the only one who makes any sense anymore, and I am so angry that we have to hide from my father and his mother. My nightmares keep me up, I don't feel like studying, Lisette thinks I am ignoring her. The only things I want to do anymore are look through my telescope and be with Cole.

In the hall he squeezed me tight and whispered in my ear, "How did it take us so long to be together?"

Yesterday on the roof, it felt like we were one. One unit of measure. One molecule made of many atoms bonded together.

Listening to him made my knees feel weak.

5/28, MIDDLE OF THE NIGHT

"This thing is serious!"

A few hours ago, we were standing in the center of the roof. I had just finished setting the telescope on the tripod mount and Cole already had his eye glued to it, adjusting the aperture, focusing the eyepiece.

"I'm looking at the moon and I can see all the rays around the Copernicus crater! It's like we could drive a truck right along the impact marks."

He was so excited. I folded my arms, smiled, and watched.

"It's crazy! If we were out in the country, where it's really dark, I'll bet we could see the Swan Nebula and maybe even the Virgo galaxy cluster with this scope!"

I touched the golden sun pendant that rested on my collarbone, and I wished my father could see how happy Cole and I were together. I think if he saw us, he really would understand.

"Can you see Neil Armstrong's footprints up there?" I teased.

"Uh-huh. Sure can. Looks like he wore a size nine and a half space boot! 'One small step for man,'" Cole put on a deep, serious news anchor voice, "'one giant step for capitalist imperialism and multinational telecommunications industries!'" He chuckled softly and managed to pull his eye away from the scope long enough to shoot me a sly grin.

I put my arms around him and leaned my head on his back as he went on looking at the moon, moving the telescope a few degrees to the right and refocusing. I took a deep breath and inhaled his intoxicating smell: earthy, like the air along Button Box Lake, mixed with the tiniest bit of something sweet, burnt sugar or caramel.

With my ear to his back, I could hear Cole's heart beating strong and steady. I sighed, gave his ribs a squeeze. "Cole Whitford," I said, "you are the best thing ever." He leaned back into my arms, still looking through the viewfinder. For a moment, I had a flash of memory that made my body go rigid. The country night sky, binoculars, the cool air beneath my nightgown. I unfocused my eyes and took in another deep breath of Cole's scent. I lifted his shirt, tasted the sweat on his back, and remembered exactly where I was. On the roof, in the city, with Cole. Exactly where I wanted to be. Doing exactly what I wanted to do.

Cole turned around in my arms as I peeled his shirt over his head. I pressed myself up against him and felt his sure hands against my skin. We kissed and everything else disappeared. The gray-orange city sky above us, the black tar roof beneath our feet—gone. I felt weightless as Cole's lips pressed against my neck, and the only sounds that remained were made by my blood pulsing through my veins, filling my ears with a rhythmic hum as every nerve ending in my body became electric with the charge that came to me from Cole.

Later, as we lay on our blanket in the shadow of the roof door, I must have dozed. I don't know how or for how long, or what I was dreaming, but when I awoke I was sitting bolt upright, Cole at my side whispering, "Atty! It's okay. We're here, on the roof. Just you and me." I looked at him and didn't know who he was. His voice was comforting; I thought about his words.

"Right," I said. "Of course. Minneapolis. The roof." I squeezed his hand and went quickly down to my apartment, remembering that my father would soon be home.

Dream:

I am in a forest and it is night. The moon is out, but it is very dark anyway, and I am scared. Not of anything in particular, but of everything. I look down on the ground and see myself lying there, dead. The me that's watching has a knife in her hand, and it's my job to skin the me on the ground as if I were a rabbit at a butcher shop. Someone is watching closely, but I don't know who it is. I start to cut my limbs off with the knife, beginning with the arms, and then I realize—I'm not actually dead. The me on the ground watches as I peel back her skin, exposing all her insides to the night air.

Memory:

I was four years old, but it's as clear as yesterday. My father hadn't been a police officer for long and still had lots of friends who weren't American cops or reporters or respectable businessmen. His friends then were people like him who'd come from far-off places where the weather was warm year-round and the ocean was something everyone had seen. Cabdrivers, office cleaners, students, salesmen. They would come to our apartment and play cards or dominoes, slapping the pieces down loudly and shouting playfully to make a point. Everyone spoke Creole unless they were directly addressing Mama, who spent most of those evenings smiling quietly and drinking cans of soda. Papa spoke to me in Creole all the time, so I understood enough to be curious. One freezing February night the house was full. I settled in to my usual spot under the glass coffee table in the living room. On the TV were pictures of men and soldiers on the streets of a country I'd never been to. The streets were made of dirt, and the houses were all low and square, painted soft pastel colors with very small windows. English mixed with French and Creole, words and names floated around the room—Aristide, coup d'état, George Bush, Baby Doc, Tonton Macoute, the Leopards. I especially remember Jean-Paul that night. He had studied pre-law with Papa back home but was now doing it all again at Metro State. He and Papa had their heads close together, talking in whispers about the country where they grew up. I fell asleep and awoke to a silent house; my father was carrying me into my room. "Sweet dreams, *ti chouchou*, I'll see you in the morning."

Fact:

The oldest radio broadcasts from the 1930s have already traveled past one hundred thousand stars.

5/28, NIGHT

It's three a.m., and I can't sleep.

I didn't tell Papa because he would have killed him and then he'd have been a criminal, a murderer. I didn't tell Mama because church and faith is what keeps her happy. I didn't tell Ms. Spencer because people would think badly of my family. I couldn't tell Rita because I had just met her. I would never tell Cole. If I told Lisette she would tell her mother, and her mother wouldn't believe me, just think worse of me.

The only thing I can do is try and forget.

5/27, EVENING

I was exhausted when I got home. I took a long shower and went to my room. I wasn't hungry. Cole had emailed me six times while I was away. Sending me songs and lyrics and even one long letter, but I couldn't look at any of them. I couldn't do anything but stand in the shower and cry until there was nothing left.

5/26, NIGHT

I am writing this by the penlight on my keychain, with my head under the covers, and I'm still worried someone will see the light through the windows; that *he* will see the light somehow and know I'm awake and up.

I have even begun to worry that he'll take away my journal, and it's really all I have keeping me sane right now. I don't want to write or say his name anymore. At first I thought I should take off right away, but then I would be leaving these kids with him. I don't have a telephone to call anyone. And who would I call anyway?

Nothing was wrong with Kelly. She doesn't have asthma. Everything he told me was a lie.

Last night I was asleep in the single cot near the bunk beds the littler kids sleep in.

Earlier that evening the sky had been clear and we had stayed up to look at the constellations. I pointed them out to the campers, passed around my binoculars. We all sat out on our sleeping bags. We sang songs.

The whole night I felt like every time I looked up he was watching me—trying to make sure I was doing the right thing, I guess. I talked about the Milky Way and explained some basic facts, and he talked about how God created the heavens and the earth.

After everyone was tucked in bed, he came around to our cabin to give me my binoculars, which I had left in the main hall. I thanked him and then he asked me to come out and show him the Equuleus constellation, said he couldn't figure out how to find the Little Horse with the binoculars. I put on a sweatshirt and followed him outside, barefoot, the smell of earth and pine everywhere and the sound of crickets.

I stood right on the steps of the cabin and held up the binoculars to focus them properly, then he said he had to get a sweater from his cabin. He asked me to come with him, and I said okay.

Now I don't know why I said okay. Why would I say okay?

Back in his cabin he took out his phone and showed me a picture of myself sleeping. A chill went through me, down to my bones. I asked him why he had it. He said because I was beautiful like an angel.

Then he showed me another picture of me sleeping. My

nightshirt was pulled up to my neck, and his hands were groping me.

My heart raced and I thought I might throw up. I turned and started to leave his room, but he got in front of me, held me by the shoulders, and said in that syrupy, friendly voice, "No, no, Atty, don't worry. I won't show this to your mother. She won't know that you do things like this. She won't know you're this kind of girl."

Then he asked me to kiss him to show that we had a deal.

I can't write the rest.

We are supposed to leave tomorrow.

5/25, DAWN

Last night someone came into the cabin. I didn't want to startle the girls, so I kept quiet but turned on the lantern, which is dimmer than the lights.

Daniel was leaning over the top bunk looking at one of the little girls in the room.

He turned when he saw me and smiled, put his finger to his lips so I wouldn't say anything.

"What's going on?" I whispered.

"Kelly was sick before we headed on the trip, and I'm checking to see how her breathing is," he said. "She has asthma. I've been praying for her."

"Oh," I said. I wondered why he hadn't told me earlier, since I was in charge of these girls.

"Can you make sure you keep an eye on her?" he asked.

"Sure," I told him.

The next day I asked Kelly how she was feeling, and she

said she was fine. She was up playing with the other girls and didn't seem sick at all.

When I told Daniel she seemed okay but that she didn't bring an inhaler with her, he said it's because the congregation was praying to clear her lungs.

I know Mama believes in prayer and says she's seen it work in the hospital. But this kind of thing seems very far-fetched.

I miss Cole. Daniel took everyone's phones at the beginning of the retreat, including mine. And I haven't been able to talk to him or get emails or messages.

Dream:

I am trying to show the little girls where to look for the Andromeda galaxy, because the sky is so dark we can actually make it out. It's not just the girls in my cabin, it's the kids from all the cabins. I do a head count to make sure none of them has wandered away. But every time I do it, it comes up different. Finally I make everyone hold hands. The little girls don't want to hold hands, but I tell them we have to until we get out of the dark. If we don't, I tell them, the sun won't come up.

Memory:

That day we watched the news together about the shooting, my mother and I waited for hours for someone to call from the precinct and tell us that Papa was alright. He had been grazed by the bullet that killed Sergeant Davis. The person they were arresting was nineteen years old; they didn't think he had a gun when they approached him. At the time I thought nineteen was grown up, but now I know how young that is for someone to be carrying a gun and killing a police officer. After that Mama said Papa should quit the force. It was the first and only fight I ever saw them have, and Papa won. He said, "I am here to protect you and Atabei. And I am here to protect our whole community. I made an oath that I'm not going to break."

Fact:
Neutron stars are so dense that just one teaspoon of what they are made of would weigh as much as the entire population on Earth.

5/24, EVENING

I am in a cabin with four ten-year-olds, a camping lantern, and this journal. The journal is so cool actually, I wonder how Papa could have thought of such a perfect gift. Even though I never see him, he always knows the perfect thing to make me happy. Seeing the pages in the dim light of the lantern, they look so rustic I could imagine I was Galileo writing by candlelight if it wasn't for the snoring little girls in bunk beds next to me.

The trip is not as bad as I thought it would be. On the bus here there was a lot of singing. Today there was a lot of making stuff with yarn. They took our phones, so I couldn't call Cole like I told him I would. It's only been twelve hours, but I am already missing him and wondering what he's doing. Imagining our nights on the roof over and over again.

Daniel is very funny, even though he talks about God

and Jesus all the time. He likes to tell me it doesn't matter if I believe in Jesus because Jesus believes in me. "That," I said, "is a logical fallacy."

I love that it doesn't make him mad when I say things like that. He just asks me more questions about the way I think and feel. It's also cool the way he listens to everything I say so intently.

Even though I don't believe this religious stuff at all I think it's interesting that people create so many different stories to explain scientific phenomena. They are looking at the same ideas from a vastly different place. I also think Daniel definitely can see things other people can't.

At dinner tonight he said, "You have a glow about you, Atty. Are you in love?" After dinner we toasted marshmallows and ate s'mores. There is a lot of candy involved in teaching the Christian faith to grade schoolers. Everyone was giddy from the sugar and laughing.

I thought about Daniel's question. Maybe it's all the God talk making me feel like this, but it's like he's watching me, even when I don't know he's there.

Dream:

It's the middle of a hot summer day, the sun is directly overhead, and I'm walking among in-between places of crisscrossing highways and off-ramps and railroad tracks. It looks like downtown east Minneapolis. It also looks like Mars. In the back of my mind I know that I have to travel a long distance, so I start to run, but my feet start to hurt. When I look down I realize that I am wearing my favorite shoes from third grade (cheap black kung fu shoes from Chinatown) that are now four sizes too small. I try to kick off the shoes, but they're stuck on my feet so I jog up a ramp that leads to I-94. Cars speed by and honk their horns. Across six lanes of traffic I can see that Cole is running also; he's going in the same direction as I am, but no matter how loudly I scream and wave my arms to get his attention—he doesn't see me. I'm running and running; it feels like the dream is going on forever, until I trip on a piece of gravel and land facedown on the shoulder. Wheels of cars are passing at my eye level, making that Doppler effect sound, and across the road I can see Cole sprinting ahead until he becomes a little dot at the end of my vision.

Memory:

I was eight or nine years old, and Mama had just gotten home from work. I walked into the kitchen sleepy and crusty-eyed, stood in the doorway blinking myself awake. Mama turned around and smiled at me. She popped open a can of Pepsi, put some oatmeal on the stove, and said, "Come, honey, sit and talk with me." The kitchen started to smell like cinnamon and warm milk, and she twisted my hair into tight braids while I sat listening to her talk about the details of her life: the boys she used to date on the reservation, the friendly nurses she worked with and the

jokes they played on each other, the cool water at her favorite swimming hole in Rainy Lake. She seemed so happy
then. I loved passing her that way—she about to go to bed
and me about to go to school with all her stories in my head.

Fact:
Saturn is the only planet in our solar system that would
float on water.

5/23, PAST MIDNIGHT

Tonight when I told Cole I was going to be gone for four days he looked so sad and a little freaked out—I immediately regretted saying I'd do the youth retreat. I asked my mother if we could call Daniel and tell him I had too much studying to do. Of course she said no, I'd already committed to it.

Once I'd finished packing and my father was asleep (Mama had left for work at the hospital), I sneaked out and up onto the roof to meet Cole. When I got up there he was lying on his back on a blanket looking up at the sky.

I lay down next to him and held his hand. The roof tar beneath us was letting out the heat of the day, and the air was thick with humidity. The sky was all gray haze and reflected back the orange glow of the city. I tried to think of something romantic to say, but all that came out was, "It's kinda gross out."

Cole laughed and looked over at me. He nudged a little closer to my side, and we lay like that for hours, holding each other, dozing and waking. I described the documentary I saw about Bonnie Parker and Clyde Barrow—how they went on a two-year crime spree across sixteen states and got caught in Louisiana on May 23 (today!), 1934.

We talked about the stars and kids at school and how strange gravity is and the way that time only exists so that everything doesn't happen at once.

5/22, SEVENTH-PERIOD STUDY HALL

In the locker room before gym, Lisette slipped me this note from Cole. He wrote it on two pieces of paper and folded it up into a tetrahedron.

Dear Atty,

Today seems like it's dragging on forever. Collins droning on about the Spanish Inquisition was torture! (Ha!)

Seriously, though, I spent most of last night awake keeping an eye on Jennifer. When I got home from school yesterday, she was nodding out on the couch. Her breathing was fine so I didn't freak out and call 9-1-1. I'd seen it before, just another day at the office. When that happens I pretty much have to make sure she doesn't pass out completely and forget to breathe, so I got out my copy of Stephen Hawking's A Brief History of Time *(classic! You've read* it, right? I'm sure you have) and found a spot within earshot where I had a good view of her. It was probably about four a.m. when I felt like I could go to sleep.

I would have blown off school, but I couldn't stand the thought of not seeing you for a whole day. Yesterday, at Rita's, I felt like I really understood how time could be accelerated or slowed down. It's like I've been looking for you all my life but didn't even realize it. I can't stop thinking about the way your hair curls around your forehead and rests on your cheek, the way you toss your head back when you laugh, the look of pure satisfaction you have when you're the only one in the room who has the right answer. Being around you gives me hope that the world might actually be a good place.

Maybe Rita's right and I need to move in with her. Maybe I need to do something so my mother will go to rehab—it's just that I have no idea what that would be.

I know that it seems hopeless right now, that your father won't let you see me and my mother is totally screwed up, but I want to be with you forever, Atty. Forever.

Last night I dreamed that we were at the North Pole, floating on a glacier, looking up at the sky. In the dream it was November, and it would be completely dark for three more months. The North Star was directly above us, and time was moving slowly and quickly at the same time. The sky looked like a time-lapse video. All the stars were swirling around that polar light, and down on the ice, it was like time was going at half speed. You were holding me, and nothing could come between us.

Let's get away from this place! I can tell Rita that I'm borrowing her car, and we can drive straight to Canada. I looked it up, and it'd take a day and a half to get to Yellowknife Park, where we could see the aurora borealis. Just you and me and the northern lights.

I love you,
cw

5/21, ABOUT TO
GO TO BED

When I got home today my head was reeling. Yesterday was a crazy roller coaster! First my father freaking out about Cole, then Cole telling me all about his mother, then the two of us, together at Rita's. I'm trying to keep it all in perspective and keep thinking like a scientist. I was in no mood to see either of my parents, so I took my time getting home. I figured that Mama would be gone and Papa would still be at work.

Instead, my father was already home, standing in the kitchen, smiling. There was takeout from Masala Walla (my favorite), a long narrow box on the kitchen table, and an open letter that had been addressed to me from the Lakeview High School principal's office.

It was a certificate saying that I was a National Merit

Scholarship finalist! And a letter saying there was still another stage to go through before winner selection.

Papa stood next to me as I read the letter. Then he handed me the box.

Inside was a Newtonian Reflector Telescope with a 6–16 millimeter zoom eyepiece!

I couldn't believe it. I turned to him nearly speechless and he pointed to the living room window, where he'd already put together the tripod with the German equatorial mount!

I felt like I'd been drowning and hadn't known it, and he'd given me a life raft!

I took the scarf off my head to let my wild white hair out, and then used the scarf to wipe my eyes.

Papa said, "I am so proud of you, *ti chouchou*. So very proud!"

We set up the telescope and pointed it out the northeastern window.

"Tell me what I'm looking at," Papa said. It was hard to get through the city's glow, but with some imagination, we could see Hydra and Leo and Ursa Major.

We brought our chickpeas and rice and lamb into the living room and ate, took turns at the telescope. "These are the things that make me happy," he said.

"Me too."

He looked so pleased. And it had been so long since I

had done anything that made him look that way.

When we were done we sat on the couch, and for some reason I started crying.

He put his arms around me.

He said, "Yesterday is gone, *ti chouchou*, today has been a long day. But tomorrow we can make a fresh start. All of us."

5/20, EVENING

We skipped school and went to Rita's house. I have never skipped school in my life, but I didn't know what to do and we needed some time to figure things out.

I could barely look at Cole as we walked down Hennepin Avenue, and it was making him anxious, making him talk more than usual. I was angry, actually angry, at him.

"What were you and my father talking about?" I asked.

"We were talking about my mother," he said.

"What? Why? Do you talk to my father every morning before I come downstairs?" I asked.

"Sometimes. He just asks how I'm doing usually."

"But you never told me you knew him. You never told me anything, I guess. Cole, what is going on?"

"Atty, I don't know what I was thinking. I . . ."

"Your mom isn't sick, is she?" I asked.

"No," he said. "She's not." He looked down at his shoe,

then directly at me. "She's a heroin addict."

The words hung in the air. I felt my heart racing in my chest after he said it. There was so much I didn't know at all. I understood him not wanting to tell me. I understood about feeling ashamed. I'd had my hunches about his mom—but I thought we were together, I thought I knew him, that we trusted each other.

"Okay," I said. "And what about what my father said about you being on probation? *Probation*, Cole!"

"I got caught buying drugs for her."

"Oh my God!"

"I had to! She was getting sick. It's not really as bad as you think. I've been doing it since I was twelve, it's only a small amount, I just got caught this time. Unfortunately, your dad was one of the arresting officers."

He was trying to sound upbeat about some of the worst things I had ever heard. He was trying to fake it with me, to be smooth like he is with everyone at school. No way was I going to listen to that. I know he's sold drugs for money before but had thought he had to because his mother was sick. But Jennifer is an addict, and he's been buying drugs for her. I get that this is where that sadness that I have always seen in him comes from. But he can't lie to me.

I turned and stared at him, shocked, angry, disgusted. But as soon as I looked at his face all my anger melted away. I couldn't stay mad at him, ever. Like he had put me under a spell.

I knew how my father felt about people who broke the law. The fact that he'd showed as much self-control as he had back by the elevators was amazing. All those warnings he used to give me about spending time with people from the building. All those warnings he gave me about people dealing and using. All I could think about was how we were going to get around Papa. In that moment I knew I would do anything to help Cole. My problems were small compared to his, my problems were over. But he was living every day with this.

"I'm in love with you," he said, and it was as though he were speaking my own thoughts. "I couldn't tell you those things because I was afraid of what you'd think."

I turned to Cole and put my arms around him, and we held each other there on the sidewalk for a long time. The only person we could think to talk to was Rita.

When we got to her house she was wearing a purple silk robe and making an omelet.

"Oh hi!" she said. "I'll make another one of these." She took eggs out of the fridge. She poured us some coffee as we told her the whole story.

"Listen," she said. "Forget about all this *Romeo and Juliet* stuff. You are your own people. You need to do what's right for yourselves. Cole, maybe it's finally time you moved in with me."

He said, "No way. You know I can't do that. She can't live all on her own. She won't even eat, what if she ODs?"

Rita looked at him with that same sad, complicated face I'd seen before.

"Baby," she said, "nobody can save a junkie, believe me, I know. I've been looking after your mom for years. She is the only one who can save herself."

I knew this was true. Cole had told me about Rita coming over, bringing groceries, cleaning the house.

"I know. I'm not trying to save her. She says when I go to college she'll go to rehab."

Rita looked at him sadly.

"I think it's true," Cole said. "I think she *will* this time."

"I thought we had a deal," she said to him. "We check in, we do what we can for her, but we don't start believing the fairy tales."

Rita kept listening and talking as she wandered around the house cleaning things up and getting dressed. She took one of her gorgeous landscape paintings off the living room wall and wrapped it in heavy paper to take somewhere.

"Listen," Rita said. "Stay here. Relax. Forget about school today. I gotta go out. There are condoms in the bathroom cupboard. Make sure you use them."

I'm pretty sure that my face turned a bright shade of magenta when Rita said that, but even before the screen door was shut behind her, Cole leaned over and kissed me so perfectly that I forgot to be embarrassed.

"Hold that thought," he said as he stood up.

I heard the door of the bathroom cabinet open and close

with a whisper, and Cole was back in my arms. How could someone's touch be so perfect? And the way that he smells! I put my hands on the inside of his shirt and lifted it gently over his head. His skin against mine was cool and smooth, with a downy line of hair that led my hand from his stomach below the button of his jeans. As our bodies wrapped together, I knew that this is how it should be. I knew how it feels to give yourself freely to someone you love—one you desire.

As the morning turned to afternoon, we held each other in a patch of sunlight stained purple from the tinted window, and Cole spoke the thoughts in my mind.

"Does this mean you forgive me?" he said.

And I couldn't help but laugh.

5/20, MORNING

S itting in Rita's living room instead of homeroom. She and Cole are in the kitchen washing dishes, so I snuck away to write this down before I forget how it went.

I tried to get out of the house in the morning without anyone seeing my hair. Papa was just getting up, Mama was just getting home from work, and they were already eating breakfast together. I had my hair all wrapped up in a scarf. If there was anything my parents disliked it was people calling attention to themselves, and they saw any sort of difference, any intentional difference, as calling attention. I had heard them talk about people in the building who they didn't like. Pierced noses! Pants worn too low! Flashy clothes! These were the kinds of crimes they saw all around them.

Mama said just last week that Lisette shouldn't wear her wolf hat because she looked like a six-year-old and was clearly trying to draw attention to herself. She always asks why we still make bead bracelets, but she stopped giving us a hard time about it after I made her one that read *Strongest Mama*. She wears it all the time.

"Oh, you look beautiful like Granme," my father said when I came into the kitchen. "Is that her scarf?"

In the photographs I'd seen, his mother was more interesting looking than beautiful—very thin and about a foot taller than me, but I was happy the scarf worked.

"It is," I said. It was. I have a lot of my grandmother's clothes from Haiti, though I never met her.

My mother looked worn-out, drinking a cup of chamomile tea, still in her scrubs and white clogs. She held her hand out to me, and I leaned close to her while she gave me a hug, then looked up at my hair. She looked closely at my forehead.

"Atty," she said. "You didn't try to cut your hair again, did you?"

"No, Mama."

Papa grabbed the newspaper to read on the bus and kissed me like he did every morning, kissed Mama, and then headed out.

She looked at me again, then reached up and pulled the scarf up on my forehead. Then she closed her eyes and shook her head.

"Atabei." She put her head in her hands and then sighed, too tired to get into a fight.

"I have to get to school," I told her. "Have a good rest."

I took an apple from the fruit bowl and rushed out. In the elevator, I took off the scarf and examined myself in the warped reflection from the stainless steel walls. Hell, yes, I thought as the doors opened on the ground floor. It's perfect.

Then I looked up and was stunned to see Cole there talking to my father.

Cole turned at the sound of the elevator doors opening, and his eyes widened. I watched my father still looking at him, taking in his expression, then turning to see me. He looked shocked and horrified. I was standing right in front of the elevator, still holding my grandmother's scarf.

They both yelled my name.

"That's so cool!" Cole said.

My father looked doubly angry that this boy was talking to me.

"Atabei," my father said. "What have you done?" He was almost trembling with rage.

"I dyed my hair, Papa. I like it this way."

"It looks better than I thought it would," Cole said.

"How do you know each other?" my father snapped.

I said "physics class" at the same time that Cole said "we're friends." And my father grabbed me by the arm and pulled me outside the building.

"Atabei, you will not spend any time with Cole Whitford. I do not want you going over to his apartment. Ever.

You will not talk to him. He is *not* your friend. Is that clear? Not now, not ever."

I was so surprised, my mouth was practically hanging open.

"Now you put that scarf back on before going to school, and we will talk about all of this later when I get home."

I remember the first thing that surprised me was that my father knew Cole's whole name. Then I was angry.

"I want to talk about it now."

"Atty, I don't have time for this. I don't want you to see that boy again, is that clear?"

"Why?" I demanded.

"Because I have arrested his mother six times in the past two years, and Cole is on probation. He is not the kind of boy you should be around. You don't know him. You think you do, but you don't. People like Cole are charming, but there is always something under the surface you can't see."

It was like a punch in the stomach. I gasped. I knew that Cole had been buying drugs and selling them to a few kids at school; he had to. His mother had no job. But the idea that he might have been caught doing it was overwhelming. Was his mother involved too?

"What is he on probation for?" I asked.

"None of your business."

5/19, NIGHT

It's Sunday and I'm lying in bed having managed to avoid my parents all day long. This morning I woke up, looked in the mirror, and decided that I needed a new look. A real EDM look, not just boring old Midwestern nerd girl who stays home and studies all the time.

In the bathroom I found the tub of Manic Panic Pastelizer Lisette had given me before her mom grounded her and banished me from their fancy house. I called her up and told her to come over and dye my hair.

"Ah, sure . . . but just to clarify . . . is it because you are trying to give your mother a *heart attack*? Get grounded until you are *thirty*? Or make sure your father forbids us from *ever* hanging out again?"

I said, "They're not home, and I'm sick of it."

"Okay," she said. "I'll be right over."

I should have done this ages ago, I thought.

Lisette came by, wearing her wolf hat and sucking on a lollipop.

"I saved you the sour-apple one," she said, handing me another sucker.

We put on Deadmau5 as loud as my neighbor used to play her music, and we mixed a color called Virgin Snow with the Pastel-izer. We left it on for two hours while we watched a YouTube video of an entire Madelin Zero show. Then listened to an old Crystal Castles album.

When we rinsed it out Lisette looked at me, stunned. I expected it would be awful and we'd have to give me the same treatment we gave her months ago.

She said, "Oh my God, Atty. It looks amazing."

I stood in front of the mirror. My hair was a pale silvery matte white. And it made my black eyes look blacker. I *loved* it.

I somehow felt like I had uncovered who I really was. I blew it dry and didn't try to rein it in like I did every morning. It was a great silver halo around my head like in a Renaissance painting.

The next thing she said was, "Your father's going to kill you."

5/18, MORNING

I realized I need a list to keep things straight.

Short term:

Win National Merit Scholarship. Being a finalist is not
good enough.

Spend more time with Lisette so she doesn't think I'm
blowing her off because I have a boyfriend.

Go to DMV to get picture for my driver's license.

Invite Cole over for dinner so Papa and Mama can meet
him.

Get tickets to Electric Daisy Carnival.

Long term:

Road trip with Lisette and Cole.

Apply early decision to Yale.

Spend whole summer at San Pedro Mártir Observatory
   in Mexico.
College.
Graduate college and travel the entire world with Cole.

5/14, NIGHT

Today instead of going up to the roof or going over to Rita's with Cole after school I suggested we go to his apartment.

At first he seemed excited about introducing me to Jennifer; he talked about things she used to do when he was little. She would take him to the lake to go swimming. They would go fossil hunting together. She always wanted to be outdoors, even in the wintertime. He told me they built a snow horse one time and poured water over it to make it into an ice horse. He had so many wonderful stories about her it made my childhood seem dull by comparison. But as we got closer to our building he got quieter and sadder.

When we got there it seemed like Jennifer was just waking up, sitting up groggily on the couch. She was not what I expected. She was thin, had long blond hair and blue eyes, acne-scarred skin. When we walked in she smiled a beautiful puzzled smile as if she weren't expecting anyone and thought it was a wonderful surprise.

The apartment was smaller than ours and had almost nothing at all in it. An old couch that looked like it had come off the street served as kind of a bed for Jennifer. A television, a table. Nothing hanging on the walls, nothing that makes a place a home. It was stuffy and smelled strange, not like smoke but like something burning. There was a pile of laundry at the foot of the couch. A sheet used as a curtain. The only thing that gave it some kind of life was a collection of stones and shells on the windowsill.

"Hey, baby," she said as Cole walked in. He went over to the couch and kissed her on the cheek, and she held his hand. She looked calm and dreamy.

"This is Atty," he said, almost as if he were talking to an old person or a child, trying to break through the mental fog.

I smiled, and she stood up unsteadily. She was wearing a skirt that looked like it had once been part of a business suit—the kind professional women wore to work—and a ribbed black tank top. Her arms and legs had a small constellation of purple bruises.

"Pleased to meet you," she said. She looked me over some more and smiled, the ghost of who she had been was clear on her face. "You *do* look awfully smart, don't you?" It was hard not to see Cole's face in hers. "Honey," she said to me, "could you do me a favor—"

But before she could finish Cole quickly told her we were going to listen to music and pulled me down a short narrow hall into his bedroom. He locked the door and apologized as soon as we got in there, but I told him it was fine.

Cole's room was the opposite of the rest of the apartment. There were constellation maps on the walls, glow-in-the-dark stars stuck to the ceiling. A tall, narrow bookcase made out of milk crates full of what looked like stolen library books, a globe, a mobile of the solar system that looked like he had made it when he was ten, a little desk with a Mac-Book on it. I marveled at all of it, and it made me like him even more. That he could create his own small world inside the depressing chaos of his mother's apartment was beautiful. He was beautiful.

He opened the laptop and put on Tiësto. And we sang along.

Oh won't you stay for awhile? I'll take you for a ride if you can keep a secret?

"That's a fancy computer," I told him. "I was hoping to get one next year."

"Ms. Spencer," he said. "She got it for me through a science scholarship program. She's the best."

He lay on the bed, and I lay next to him with my head on his shoulder.

I stared up at the papier-mâché planets hanging from the mobile and thought about how strong he must be—taking care of himself and taking care of his mother, who seemed not to be able to do much of anything for herself.

"I'm sorry that I brought you here," he said with a distant stare.

I was confused. Was he saying that he didn't like me anymore?

"You'll probably never want to talk to me again, now that you've seen Jennifer."

I looked at him and put my hand on his cheek, closed my eyes, and kissed his lips. "I always want to talk to you. I want to be with you always."

Then I felt the tension break and the rush of relief as it radiated from his skin. He held me tight.

"I thought once you saw all this you would leave."

"No way," I said. "Never."

And I thought again about our times together on the roof and at Rita's house, talking, listening to music, holding hands, and I knew that Cole had something that could transform me. I put my hand up inside his shirt to feel his warm skin, and knew I could stay like that forever, with him holding me, his hand in my hair, listening to his heart beating.

No matter what was going on outside, we had our bubble, our own planet, our own atmosphere.

5/13, AFTER BREAKFAST

L isette slept over last night, and we stayed up and watched movies and ate a whole bag of Sour Patch candy and made bead bracelets.

"It's weird how something we did when we were, like, eight years old is cool again," she said.

"Um. Like eating Sour Patch candy ever goes out of style?" I said.

She had nearly a whole forearm full of kandi and it looked great, colorful. She has the whole look now—the fur boots, the wolf hat, glitter makeup. She looks like some kind of primitive space animal. And it totally does feel like playing dress-up like when we were little, but also like some amazing performance art. Maybe I'll dye my hair too.

"The thing is," Lisette said. "I feel like, from looking at all the YouTube videos, that a lot of people who go to Electric Daisy and Ultra are not that smart—but then I read an article that said people with the highest IQs listen to trance music. Here, give me that. Why do you have such a hard time with these knots?"

I handed her the bracelet I was making.

"I mean that's true even anecdotally," I said. "Who listens to EDM at our school? If you look at just you, me, and Cole, you've got the kids with the two highest SAT scores and a tall spacewoman with perfect teeth."

"I was wondering how long it would take you to bring up that test again. I think it's been like five hours since you mentioned it," she said. "Anyway, my alien knowledge makes up for my lack of SAT scores."

She handed me a bracelet she'd made for me.

All heart-shaped red beads, and the words *Gravity's Angel* in the center.

We talked for so long last night, trying to strategize a trip to EDC, about how amazing it would be to go on a roller coaster or sit on a Ferris wheel while listening to trance. Whoever thought those kinds of things up was definitely one of us.

I love spending time with Lisette. She knows how to have a good time. I love Cole too. But there is so much less drama hanging out with other girls.

5/11, AFTER DINNER

This week was probably the most fun I have ever had at school, being with Cole every day and working on astronomical maps together in Ms. Spencer's class. He can draw really well, and he knows his stuff when it comes to dark matter. At lunch he and I and Lisette sat together instead of just me and Lisette slinking away to the art room like we usually do.

I've gotten over being angry at him for selling drugs to that crowd. Apparently his mom is sick and can't work. It's true that those kids are losers, but I've been paying attention to how Cole acts with them—he really isn't their friend, he really is different. I just hope he doesn't get caught and get into some real-world trouble.

Oh my God. But more important: Lisette is making this *insane* shirt out of fake fingernails! It sounds gross and weird but actually it looks so, so, so cool. She said it's the perfect thing to wear with her fur boots and wolf hat. She said she's going to wear that outfit to the Electric Daisy Carnival, if we ever figure out a way to convince our parents to let us go. Or figure out a way to get in.

"It's good to have goals," I said.

"It's better to have conspiracies!" Lisette said.

After school on Monday, the three of us were walking around and going a little bit out of our minds, when Lisette said, "Let's go to the Mall of America!" Cole rolled his eyes.

"You want to go *shopping*?" I asked her.

"No. But Amazing Mirror Maze? C'mon."

"What will we do there?" Cole asked.

"Haven't you been to the mall?" Lisette asked.

"Uh, no," he said.

"Won't your mom say no?"

"No to shopping?" Lisette asked. "Atty, c'mon."

We hopped on the Blue Line and crammed into a corner. Usually this time of day I am alone in my room studying with my headphones on. Sitting with Cole and Lisette—my two favorite people—leaned up against me on the train ride made me kind of giddy, and everything Lisette said was, as always, funny. Me and Cole are so dark and heavy, but that girl is probably the funniest person in the universe.

Taking Cole into the mall was like leading an alien around. Lisette kept asking him if he was high.

"Uh, I don't think I have to be high to be weirded out by a place called Alpaca Connection, especially when I'm breathing recirculated air from millions of suburban Mid-westerners on antidepressants. I mean, the mall has its own gift shop with things that just say Mall of America on it! Seriously? I can't . . . How is this a thing?"

We walked past a place called Hat World.

Cole had a look of such horror on his face it made me laugh.

"Is this place a big social science experiment or some-thing?" he asked. "We're supposed to see how fast capitalism can erode our reasoning?"

A tour group—led by a tall man wearing a headset and holding up a little Swedish flag—walked by us. Cole looked incredulous, started to say something but stuttered and eventually gave up, and Lisette pointed at him, burst out laughing.

Then: Amazing Mirror Maze. Cole did not bump into one thing! He did not get lost! He walked straight through! He must be the only person on Earth who has achieved this. We could hear Lisette calling out to us from some-where in the middle, then various "ows" and "sorrys" then "oh shit" and "where the hell are you guys?"

It took me almost as long as Lisette to get out. When I did, Cole was leaning on the rail in front of the exit, his backpack at his feet, reading *God Created the Integers* by Ste-phen Hawking.

Finally Lisette emerged, grinning.

"There's a little pit of narcissists in the center of that

thing combing their hair and checking out their biceps," she said.

I looked behind her and recognized the kids she was talking about coming out of the maze. Cole used to hang out with some of them all the time: Jason Sanchez, Steve O'Connor, John Newman, and a couple of other kids whose names I couldn't remember. Steve came over and looked at the three of us.

"Hey, Cole. Honor Society meeting at the mall today?" Up close I could see that his pupils were huge and his arm was bouncing absently at his side.

"Yeah, y'know, sometimes the conference room at the American Association for the Advancement of Science is closed, so we have to slum it out here." Cole was smiling, but I could tell that he was hoping this would end quickly.

"Ri-i-ight . . ." Steve ran his hand through his dark wavy hair and looked from me to Lisette and back to Cole. "I didn't know that it was costume day at the mirror maze, or I would have dressed up too."

"Fuck off, O'Connor. You dumb-ass speed freak." Lisette has hated him ever since he put gum on the seat of her chair in Mr. Dotz's ninth-grade algebra class. And it's true that he really is a shithead. It's beyond me why Cole would even give that kid the time of day.

"Ooh, you sure are touchy there, Wolfy."

Lisette is about three inches taller than Steve O'Connor and played field hockey every weekend for years until this fall. I've seen her take down girls twice her weight, and when she took a step forward I thought for sure she was going to haul off and crack him in the nose. But Cole slipped in between them, ignoring the exchange.

"Funny running into you here, bro. But we're gonna be late for the six o'clock meeting of the Twin Cities Unicycle Club if we don't head out right now. See you tomorrow in homeroom." He linked one arm in mine and one in Lisette's and walked toward the escalator.

"I could murder that clown!" Lisette said under her breath as she pulled her arm away from Cole. "How do you even talk to that guy?"

"Yeah, he can be an ass. But . . ."

"But nothing, dude. I heard that you're the one who sells him his pills—true or false?"

Cole paused for a second and looked at me from the corner of his eye.

"True," he said. We walked toward the exit, and he went on. "I don't like them and I don't like doing it, but, Lisette, you could never understand how it is."

"That's for sure."

5/8, AFTER SCHOOL

The pastor called my mother and asked specifically that I come on the youth retreat. He said there would be younger kids who would need a chaperone and that I could also teach them about the constellations so they could "better appreciate God's majesty."

I told her I couldn't teach anyone that stars were a part of God's majesty. And that Neil deGrasse Tyson would throw up if he ever heard of someone doing such a thing.

She told me to take my headphones off and stop shouting at her.

"He's going to pay you to chaperone," she said. "And you might get to the observatory again, who knows?"

"I need to study," I said.

"You can study when the children are asleep," she said.

Papa came in from the living room. "If she doesn't want

to go, she doesn't have to."

"No, it's okay," I said, partly to make my mother feel bad and partly to make her feel proud of me. "I'll go."

What's the worst that could happen?

5/6, AFTERNOON

This morning when I got off the elevator, Cole just took my hand right away and we started walking to the bus stop.

"Rita is so cool," I told him.

"The coolest," he said. "Sorry about that girlfriend comment, she's like that."

I felt my heart sink. He was holding my hand but apologizing that someone had called me his girlfriend. It made me feel all twisted up inside. We were so happy yesterday afternoon, but maybe he had second thoughts.

"That's okay," I whispered.

He stopped walking and turned to me; he was almost trembling.

"Okay like how?" he asked.

"Okay that she said that."

His cheeks were flushed, and he looked like he wanted me to go on.

"Okay that she said that . . ." I almost couldn't finish. "Because I want to be your girlfriend."

The smile that broke over his face was one of the most beautiful things I'd ever seen.

We walked the rest of the way to the bus stop and held hands on the bus and walked that way into the school. I thought people would be looking at us. But Lisette was the only one who really noticed.

Her mother had taken her to the hairdresser to try and fix what we had done. It must have cost a fortune. But Lisette hated it. She Snapchatted me all the details from the hairdresser, including a selfie of her crying when the job was totally done. She was wearing a hat that looked like a wolf head to cover it.

She ran up to us in the hall.

"Nerds in love!" she teased. "What will Ms. Spencer say?" She paused and her face darkened for a second. "You can't steal Atty from me," she said to Cole, and he raised both arms in a gesture of surrender. A smile spread slowly across his face, and he raised the thick line of his eyebrows in a "Who me?" kind of expression.

"I'm serious!" Lisette said.

Cole's look turned warm and calm, his fine lips pursed pleasantly.

"I promise," he said, one hand still half raised at his side.

The rest of the day was a blur I was so happy.

5/5, NIGHT

Cole's mother is still sick. But today he looked rested. After school he met me at the chemistry lab and asked if I wanted to come over to Rita's with him. It made me a little sad to think that he was introducing me to her—like despite all the flirting he was definitely saying that he and I are just friends.

"Will she mind?"

"Why would she mind? I've been telling her all about you, she wants to meet you!"

It was only three o'clock. "Will she be home from school yet?"

He laughed.

We didn't take the bus but walked all the way down to Lake Street. The trees all had little green buds on them, and small brown and black sparrows were hopping around crazily on the lawns and bushes and trees like they had been waiting all winter for today! Cole jumped up in the air when a tree branch hung low, tried to swing on it, or pluck a leaf, or pull it down.

My heart was beating so fast I was afraid he'd be able to see it pounding right through my T-shirt—the black one with the Above & Beyond lyric on it in big white letters: YOU WERE THE SUN AND MOON TO ME. And just when I was thinking that, a sparrow came flying straight at us only a foot or two above our heads! I jumped to the side with an embarrassing yelp at the same time that Cole jumped up and tried to grab it—narrowly missing!

"What were you going to do if you caught it?" I laughed at him.

"Let you hold it in your hands!" he said, his voice full of energy. "So you could feel its little heart beating four hundred sixty times a minute. Can you believe that—seven and a half times a *second*! And that's at rest!" He was smiling and shaking his head incredulously.

I thought I would melt into the sidewalk right in that spot.

Eventually we got to Rita's house on Harriet Avenue South and went around to the side door. In the yard was a weird old sculpture of an owl made with beer cans and driftwood and wire. Cole reached behind the sculpture and pulled out a key, then unlocked the door. We walked into a hallway that was hung with purple tapestries that had little round mirrors sewed into them. The house smelled like burnt sugar. We walked farther into a cozy, cluttered living room where an enormous almost white painting hung over the couch. But after a minute, I could see shapes of brushy pale blues and strange grays and light pinks. It was hard to say exactly what it was a picture of—when I looked at it, I could feel the wind roaring off of the lakes in the winter. I shivered and couldn't stop staring.

"Ah . . . ," Cole said as he watched me looking at it. "She paints these." He gestured around the room, and I noticed there were three more.

"Anybody home?" Cole called.

"Cole!" A woman, who I assumed was Rita's mom, came out holding a little torch, the kind we sometimes use in chemistry class. She was thin and had an angular, weathered face, was wearing bright-red lipstick and a short black dress. She wore many bangle bracelets. Had salt-and-pepper hair held up in a silver clip that looked like a bird skull. She gave him a quick kiss on the cheek.

"Come in, I'm having a hell of a time making the top of the crème brûlée. Maybe you can do it." She lowered her voice a bit as if the next sentence was meant only for him. "I wanted to have something fancy for the special occasion."

She turned to me. "You must be Atty." She gave me a big hug, then pulled back and looked at my face, smiling. "I'm Rita."

I probably looked as shocked as I felt.

She said, "You okay?"

"I thought you were a kid, I mean—before I met you," I said. "Like our age." All the stories Cole had told me were about him and Rita listening to music or studying or building weird sculptures in her yard, and it never occurred to me that she was not our age.

She started laughing. "Well, inside maybe, but . . . Come in, come in."

The windowsills in her kitchen were filled with knick-knacks. The kitchen itself was a mess, dishes and pans in the sink, cabinet doors flung open. There were several pastry tins of custard lined up on the counter and a bag of sugar next to them.

Rita handed me the crème brûlée torch. "Your girl-friend's good at science, right?" she asked Cole. I felt a sudden cringing excitement when she said the word *girl-friend*, like I almost couldn't breathe and I couldn't look at Cole. I was waiting for him to say I wasn't his girlfriend.

"And you're French too, right?" Rita asked me. Her eyes were bright and blue.

Cole was grinning at both of us.

"Ah . . . my father's Haitian," I said.

"Well close enough."

She poured a layer of sugar over the custard, and I held the torch above it trying to get the right angle to melt it. It was surprisingly satisfying watching the sugar change form.

I handed the torch to Cole so he could do the next one, and his fingers brushed mine and I could feel a pull between us, like a quiet weight was pressing us together.

When we were done we went out and sat on Rita's screened-in porch and ate crème brûlée and drank coffee.

Rita asked me a million questions about trance music, and then she brought out all her old cassette tapes and we listened to them. She had Patti Smith, Prince, and the Clash, and David Bowie, Parliament, and tons of jazz: John Coltrane, Miles Davis, Ornette Coleman. She had good taste in music for an old person. She asked me how Cole and I met, and then I asked *her* how Cole and she met.

"In the delivery room the day he was born!" she said, laughing.

"Rita is my mom's best friend," Cole said quietly.

The two exchanged a look that was sad and strange and that I didn't understand.

"How's she doing?" Rita asked.

"Better today," Cole said. And I wondered if his mother had some terrible disease.

"Has she been to the doctors?" I asked.

Rita gave Cole a loving look.

"Many times," she said.

5/3, AFTER SCHOOL

This morning when I woke up there was no email from Cole, and when he met me at the elevator he looked tired and was wearing the same clothes he had on the day before.

"Are you alright?" I asked him.

"I'm fine," he said. "My mother was sick and I was up with her last night."

He smiled, and almost like a reflex he reached out and took my hand.

I immediately felt my heart flutter as his skin touched my skin. And I could feel how much he wanted to touch my hand, like he needed it more than anything in the world.

Dream:
It is night and I am walking through the beautiful woods. The air is clean and smooth and when I look up, I can see clusters of stars peeking through the tree branches. I've

walked far, but I am not tired at all. The ground begins to slowly slope upward, and I feel my calf muscles flexing as I walk. The trees become thinner the higher up that I go, and I can see more and more of the sky. I have the feeling of being completely alone and completely at ease until I reach the top of a very high mountain, where I climb a large smooth boulder. I have been walking for hours. I am not fatigued. At my feet there is a perfectly round hole with no light inside. I understand why I have been climbing and I step into the hole and float down in a free fall until I open my eyes and I'm in my room, the window shade glowing orange with the beginning of day.

Memory:

I've been trying to figure out the first real memory that I have, not just one that I remember from pictures. I'm pretty sure it's this: It's winter, I'm all bundled up in some kind of toddler suit and lying on my back on the living room floor. The sun is shining in through the window and dust motes are floating around looking like thousands of shimmering stars. I wondered—how did all those sparkling beings get to be here?

Fact:

Space is only sixty-two miles above the Earth. If you could drive a car straight up, you would be there in an hour.

5/1, AFTER DINNER

Scores are back for the SAT. Math 760, reading and writing 640. I would have liked higher than a 1400, but you can't say that to other people without seeming like a jerk. Lisette got a 1240, which is very good. Ms. Spencer told me not to worry because I will likely be a National Merit Scholar, but I think I need to dedicate at least another ten hours of study to make sure I raise the low score. I asked her if she knew if anyone else got 1400 or better, and she said one other person in class did. Cole! Of course.

Still, I went home feeling like I should have done better.

Back in Haiti, Papa studied at the Université Notre Dame in Port-au-Prince. His plan was to go to law school in the United States, but that didn't work out so well. Before Papa came along and went to university, the whole Taton family were sugarcane vendors.

Mama is not so interested in higher education. Unless

it's me doing well in school. You have to be smart to be an emergency room nurse, though, and I can't think of anyone else I would want around me in an emergency.

I told my mother when I become an astrophysicist or an astronomer they won't have to work anymore and I will buy them a house in Minnetonka. And she said, "Atty, we love our work."

I was like, "Then why are you always telling me I should do something better?"

"We love that work," she said. "You love studying. You love astronomy."

I know my mother loves her work as much as she loves Jesus. But Papa I'm not sure about. And I don't know how they can go without seeing each other for so long. Sometimes Papa is just getting home when Mama is leaving for her shift. On Saturdays they both have off, but otherwise I think they spend about eight hours a week together at the most. Mama is always telling me how lucky they are to have such a responsible daughter. But I think it's because she feels guilty they aren't around. When she says it I feel guilty because when they're gone I have Lisette over and we sip Papa's rum, make bracelets, listen to trance music, and watch videos of EDM festivals. Nothing is supposed to distract from my schoolwork. Maybe that's why I got a low grade on the writing.

I'm sure this is not the kind of thing Papa wanted me to be writing about when he bought me this journal.

4/29, DAYBREAK

Every day I wake up early to check my email and find Cole has sent me another song. Then when I get off the elevator he is there and we walk to the bus together. I still haven't met Rita, but he talks about her all the time. I don't think she goes to our school. Either way he sent me these words last night and an old Daft Punk video:

We've come too far to give up who we are
so let's raise the bar and our cups to the stars.

Dream:
I dreamed I was taking a test, but the tip of my pencil kept breaking. In the end I had to sharpen it with my teeth.

Memory:

This must have been fifth grade. When I got home from school my mother was already there, and she was watching the news, very quiet and sad. I stood next to her and watched, and they showed a scene by a building that looked like the one we lived in but was somewhere else in the city. And there was yellow crime scene tape around and police cars and then I heard the newscaster say that two police officers had been shot and one was killed.

I ran to my mother and started crying. "Is it Papa? Is it Papa?"

She walked to the refrigerator and grabbed a can of soda. She looked completely stunned. Then she put her arms around me. "We don't know yet, Atty. So we are going to pray."

Fact:

The Hercules starburst looks tiny in the sky, but it is the home of hundreds of thousands of stars.

4/27, EVENING

Wow. This is really happening! I got this email from Cole Whitford today. It looks like he sent it at 2:48 a.m. last night!

Dear Atty,

Thanks for the education! I've spent the past three hours listening to songs off YouTube, making playlists, and having my mind blown apart. Here's a playlist that I made. Tell me what you think!

Galantis: "Runaway"
Martin Garrix: "Don't Look Down"
Axwell /\ Ingrosso: "Something New"
Shapov: "Disco Tufli" and "Party People"
A-Trak: "Push"
Fox Stevenson: "Sweets (Soda Pop)"

Nero: "The Thrill"

Tiësto: "The Only Way Is Up"

I'll see you later in school. Maybe we can ask Ms. Spencer to make us lab partners for the next experiment in physics class?

cw

Of course I didn't say a thing to anyone about it. But it must be written all over my face. Daniel was over to visit my mother and kept looking at me funny.

"What's on your mind, Atty?" he said.

4/26, ALMOST MIDNIGHT

I can't believe the night I just had!

I went onto the roof again to the side where I can get the best look at the Perseus double cluster. (Light pollution is bad, but sometimes when it's clear . . .) And he was there! Cole. He was there actually sitting on the ledge of the building with his feet hanging over the side. I had no idea who it was from the back and for a minute I was afraid my father was right that it's dangerous to go up there, and I was also afraid if I said anything he would startle and might fall. I pulled my headphones off and let them hang around my neck.

He must have heard the music because he turned.

"Hi," he said.

"Hi," I said. "What are you doing on the roof of my building?"

"It's my building too. We moved here last week," he said. "Fourth floor."

"Wow," I said. "I never saw a moving van or anything."

"Yeah, we"—he paused a second like he wasn't sure what to say—"we don't like to have a lot of material things," he said. "What are you listening to?" He turned all the way around and sat with his back against the inside wall of the ledge.

I took off the headphones and handed them to him. It was DJ Mercer. He's French, but most of what he samples is in English. Cole put the headphones on, and his eyes grew wide.

"What *is* this?" he asked.

"This is just the tip of the iceberg," I told him. I scrolled through my playlists and put on some Skrillex.

Cole said, "I can't believe this, I've never heard anything like it."

And I could tell by looking at him that the music was doing the same thing to him it had done to me. Putting things in order, making you think about complex things fitting together. How the stars align.

"What the hell is this called?"

"It's EDM—electronic dance music. Trance, actually," I said. "I thought you listened to this kind of stuff. I saw you wearing glow bracelets at the observatory the other day." My face felt flushed as I admitted that I'd noticed him.

He laughed and got a big smile on his face. His bottom teeth were crooked. "Those were Rita's."

"Oh," I said. I didn't know who Rita was, but I assumed it was his girlfriend. Either way it didn't matter because I have a friend in the building now.

We spent the rest of the night trading headphones and binoculars and talking about Ms. Spencer's class; the way that she gets so excited about time and space and motion, and how she really listens when you're speaking to her. And how every once in a while you can hear a slight lisp when she says words with the letter *s* in them.

"You're so cool, Atty," he said. And it actually made me laugh out loud because no one in the history of the universe has ever said anything like that to me, let alone Cole Whitford.

At eleven, I ran back downstairs because my father would be getting home soon and I had to pretend I was asleep. He doesn't know how much time I spend on the roof. He doesn't know I go to the roof at all.

4/24, EARLY MORNING

I wish I could say that I am not lonely. I wish I could say that being an only child is a good thing, but it doesn't feel like a good thing these days. My mother and Pastor White want me to go on a Christian youth retreat. They're having it at the state park near the Casby Observatory and so I'm actually thinking about it. I can't imagine the kinds of kids who go on Christian youth retreats.

But Mama desperately wants me to be one of them. She even brought Pastor White over for coffee on one of her days off so he could convince me in person. He's friendly and seems cool. Before he left, he insisted that we should start calling him Daniel, because "we're all a part of the same church family." It feels weird, like something is out of place, but he's young for a minister, so I guess it kind of makes sense that he's not too concerned with the "respect your elders" thing.

It is an understatement to say that my father is stressed by work. He is so paranoid after getting back from patrol, so frightened that something is going to happen to me, he sometimes won't let me leave the building. And he doesn't want me to hang out with other people who live in the building. And he won't tell me why he's so freaked out or what happened. When I asked why we don't just move he said moving was the plan and that he and my mom are saving so we can do it.

And then he gave me the "you will go to college and become a famous scientist" speech, He said I won't have to live like him and my mother. "Papa," I told him. "There's nothing wrong with the way you grew up or the way we live now."

This year his schedule has been better, though he's still not home very much. He *is* home for *Cosmos*. So we watch Neil deGrasse Tyson together. The other day he actually said to me, "*Ti chouchou*, after college you can marry a man like that." I just rolled my eyes and let out a short laugh.

"Only not as chubby as Neil," I said.

"Definitely not as chubby," Papa said.

Last night, though, both my parents worked until late and I went up on the roof with my binoculars. There's a chair up there, and an ashtray and some empty beer cans, and there's always light pollution, but you can still make out the constellations if you know what you're looking for.

4/22, AFTER SCHOOL

On Monday Lisette wore a hat. She apologized for her mother freaking out.

"She has to let you come over again because otherwise I'll fail science."

"You won't fail."

"I'll get a C, which is the same as failing for them, and then I'll be grounded again."

Lisette is one of the only people who gets it about having those kinds of parents, where the worst thing you could do is get a bad grade. If your mark falls in anything they start to think about what to take away from you. School is easy, and it's hard to get a bad mark. But it's still annoying to have them tell you all the time how that's what matters. Sometimes it's more than annoying to think that your grades are why they like you or think you're special.

We sat in the lunchroom at the corner table by the back

exit drinking chocolate milk, which is what we'd done since we were in middle school together.

"So, Cole Whitford can talk," Lisette said. "Tell me about it."

Then before I could say anything she said, "Oh my God, look at your face! You are totally crushing on him. Atty, what the hell?"

"I think he likes astronomy," I said.

"But he's such a douche bag!"

"I think he might actually be okay."

"And his friends! Not only are those guys morons, they're stoned, like, all the time. I heard that Cole Whitford is the one who gets the drugs for them."

"Yeah, they're messed up, but he's smart—I know because he's the only one besides me who ever knows anything in physics class. I don't know about him dealing, but he never looks stoned to me. Never."

"Why is it all the messed-up boys are so beautiful?"

"He's smart!" I said again.

"Atty," she said. "He's hot."

4/19, NIGHT

The thing about Lisette being grounded is that I have literally no one else to talk to. I went to church with my mother this morning. My father has the convenient excuse that he is patrolling on Sunday. I actually don't mind church that much. It's a pretty building, and it smells good. And it makes my mother happy to be there. It means a lot to her. So far she hasn't tried to make me accept Jesus into my heart. And the pastor at her church, Pastor White, is always happy to see me.

He mostly asks questions. Like today.

"Your mom tells me you want to be a scientist," he said. "I suppose you're not very interested in religion."

I said, "Not really."

"Me neither," he said.

I looked at him skeptically.

"I'll tell you why," he said. "It's not a religion, it's a

relationship. Jesus's love reaches, pursues, and *remains*. There is nowhere you can go where Jesus's love won't find you, Atty. Now you tell me something about science."

"Only fifty-five percent of Americans know the sun is a star," I told him.

"So you and I both have our work cut out for us," he said. "I'd like to talk to you more about it sometime."

And maybe we will. I like talking when people seem genuinely interested in what I have to say.

4/18, NIGHT

Oh my GOD. Total disaster!

Today I went over to Lisette's to help her dye her hair. She bought a big tub of Manic Panic Pastel-izer (she read about it in *Allure* magazine) and a color called Voodoo Blue. And we mixed them up until they were this beautiful pale electric color and then I put on rubber kitchen gloves and rubbed the stuff all over her head. We brought her speakers into the bathroom and were listening to Dash Berlin and looking up the dates for Electric Daisy Carnival in Las Vegas while we waited to rinse it out.

It did not look anything like the pictures of girls in *Allure* when we were done.

I was just like, "Let's add more blue, it will be fine," but Lisette decided we should cut it into a better style. The only scissors we had were sewing shears. She said she wanted bangs—she really did. But as soon as I made the first cut I knew that it would be awful. Bangs are never an improvement for people with long hair because they make you look insane. A bob with bangs makes you look like a preppy girl who just decided to put in a wash-out color, or a chemo patient wearing a wig. And so in the end we gave her a short, choppy almost pixie cut, which looked very cute with her pointy chin. And we were so happy about it. Until her mother came home and completely flipped her shit.

"What the hell is going on? Oh my God, Lissy. What have you *done*?"

"We're fixing each other's hair," Lisette told her.

"Oh. So you put that topknot in Atty's hair, and then she shaved your goddamn head?" She was really angry. She was looking at the pile of pastel-blue hair in the trash can and starting to cry.

I started to say something, and she turned around and glared at me.

"Atty, how could you *do* this?"

"It wasn't Atty," Lisette yelled.

"Who was it then? Who is it that comes up with ideas like this? You know full well Atty would never let you dye her hair or cut it, or do anything of the sort. Atty's parents would never allow such a thing. You are grounded! Give me your phone. Atty, you are going home right now!"

Lisette rolled her eyes, gave me the tub of Pastel-izer, and I left before her mom could blame me for anything else.

4/18, MORNING

I've been thinking since Thursday about Cole Whitford. Even though we didn't really talk at the trip to Casby. I've been thinking about his glow-in-the-dark bracelets and wondering if he listens to EDM. There are maybe four people I know at school who do—and two of them are just pretending to like it, so they have an excuse to look weird.

After the trip I called Lisette and asked her if Cole was going out with anyone.

She was like, "Cole Whitford? Who doesn't talk?"

"He talked to me," I said.

I could almost hear her shrug over the phone. "Come over and help me dye my hair," she said. "I guess you'd better tell me about the boy who's stealing you away from me."

4/17, ALMOST NOON

It's Friday morning, but I get to have the day off since we got back so late last night. Sitting alone at home, feeling a little dazed, listening to Lisette's favorite mix.

I was ten when I first heard Daft Punk; our neighbor was playing it and I could hear through the wall of my bedroom. The walls are so thin here. It would drive my mother crazy. Crazier, I should say. Mama would get home from her shift exhausted, and the neighbor would just be waking up, putting on music while she got dressed or whatever it was she did. And she had parties too. The music thumping through the wall, louder in my room than anywhere else. She also put it on in the afternoon.

My parents were angry, thinking I wouldn't be able to study. But I have never had trouble concentrating. In fact it seems like the more going on, the easier it is for me to think. I used to love that I could hear her music through the wall when I got home from school, because it was better than silence and nobody home. And electronic music was the perfect thing to have on in the background while I did homework; it made me want to work harder. Sometimes I would watch episodes of *Cosmos*, listen to my neighbor's music through the wall, listen to Skrillex on YouTube, and do my homework at the same time. It felt like the perfect combination of sounds and ideas and images. It's weird to say, but it made me focus. Daft Punk's "Technologic" was the first song I downloaded.

Eventually my father gave the neighbor so many noise ordinance tickets she stopped playing her music, but by that time I had a pair of headphones and my own music.

I got good grades, and they never asked me what I was listening to. They were tired and busy, and happy that the noise had stopped.

4/17, DAWN

Dream:

I am on a bus going to the ocean. I've never seen the ocean, so I am excited. I have a toy boat with me that I plan on getting into and sailing away in once we get there.

Memory:

When I was twelve we went to visit my grandmother at Red Lake Nation. My mother didn't tell me why we were going, but when we got there it turned out it was because my grandfather was back. He had left the reservation when my mother was a girl, and people thought for a long time he might be dead, but now he was back and old and had moved in again with my grandmother.

Grandma was cooking in the kitchen and acted like she didn't notice him. And my grandfather was sitting in the living room; it looked like he was half asleep. He was thin and looked very strong, and he had a tattoo of a bird on his forearm. I sat near him with my mother and my aunts, and nobody talked and the air felt tight and strange. The smell of my grandma's food was heavy and delicious in the room.

"Where did he go?" I asked my mom.

She shushed me.

My grandfather looked up. His eyes were kind and black.

"For a really long walk," he said.

My mother and my aunts started laughing.

Grandma leaned her head through the door. She looked at him and then us.

"He tell you he went for a walk?" she said.

Fact:

The atmosphere on Earth is proportionally thinner than the skin on an apple.

4/16, NIGHT

When I woke up this morning there were two wrapped boxes on the kitchen table. The first was small and inside was a necklace with a tiny golden sun on it.

The second was this journal. My parents were already at work, but Papa left this letter on the table.

Happy birthday, ti chouchou. *This book is for you to put down your dreams and memories and the facts you want to record. Someday, when you become a famous astronomer, people will want to read about your life and see your notes.*

It couldn't have been a better start to an even better day. It's midnight now, and I just got home because today was our field trip to Casby Observatory, which has the largest refracting telescope in the state! Fifteen of us from Ms. Spencer's class went. The place was amazing, surrounded by woods! And it was a perfect night because there was steady air. This was the first time I had ever been in a dome observatory and the first time I ever used such a powerful telescope. You could see the polar ice caps on Mars! And the planet didn't look red but more like the color of butterscotch candy. And the stars were so bright, like I'd never seen them in my entire life.

Outside it was clear and crisp and smelled amazing like pine. I love the woods. After my turn at the scope I went outside to look up at the sky, and there was a boy from my class sitting under the one little lamp that hung above the bench near the back door. Cole Whitford. His hair was down to his shoulders and looked gold in the halogen light. He was wearing glow-in-the-dark bracelets. We had never talked before and I didn't think he even knew my name, but he looked up and smiled at me.

"Just before you got here," he said, "I saw a shooting star."

Acknowledgments

Thank you to my editor, Claudia Gabel, and to Alex Arnold and the fantastic team at Katherine Tegen Books. Working with such dedicated professionals is a pleasure that continues to grow with each project. I am grateful to my stalwart group of first readers and most lovingly critical audience: the elusive Claire Kittridge, and the always eager Dove and Zane. I couldn't have done it without you.